WHISPER MY NAME

ASPEN GOLD SERIES BOOK 13

CHERYL ST.JOHN

Cover and interior design by Cat & Doxie Author Services

❀ Created with Vellum

Dedicated to Gigi, whose birth gave me the opportunity to nurture and love her. That wonderful and exhausting fifteen months refreshed my mojo so that I could write with renewed energy. During that precious time, I promised myself that from now on I will only write books I love.

WHISPER MY NAME

She was the girl behind the headlines

Laurel Whitaker has been her name for fifteen years. Anyone
hearing her true identity would know who she was, and she's
had enough of cameras, questions and stares. Spencer,
Colorado is a great place to blend in among the tourists. But
unwanted attention comes in the worst possible form—a
tough, perceptive, and all too determined lawman.

Sheriff Joe Cavanaugh looks out for people—his large loving
family, his teenage daughter, anyone in his county who needs
him. But the mistrustful young woman staying in the lake
house beside his property goes out of her way to avoid his
help, and that's suspicious. Instinct tells him she's hiding
something…and attraction motivates him to uncover her
secrets.

Will Laurel's truth be his undoing…or hers?

CHAPTER ONE

Spencer, Colorado
Mid-November

*L*aurel Whitaker could count on one hand the number of people she'd spoken with in the six months she'd been in Spencer. The only person she talked to with regularity was Dr. Bella Easton, whose office was on the third floor of the Medical Building that sat behind Edna Burnham Memorial Hospital. Laurel visited at 10 a.m. the second Tuesday of every month. Today as usual, she made herself a cup of salted caramel coffee and inhaled the aroma before putting on the plastic lid and taking a seat.

"Lovely dress," Dr. Easton said with a smile. "Ordered it online, didn't you?"

Laurel took a sip of the strong brew, the coping mechanism of routine keeping her centered. "I did."

Dr. Easton smiled. She was a tall, slender woman, probably in her early forties, with short-cropped hair who usually dressed in slacks and a lightweight cardigan. She seemed to have a fondness for greens and corals. Laurel was comfortable in her office and found her easy to talk with. "Last month I suggested it was time for you to start getting acquainted with the community. How have you done with that?"

"I had a conversation with the cashier at Martin's Grocery. We talked about how chilly it had been overnight. And I walked inside the bank to handle my transaction." Even though she could have used the drive-up window without undue duress. "The teller was wearing a blue blouse."

The doctor had suggested she needed to take these confidence-building steps. A social media advisor and manager with social anxiety might be ironically humorous, but Laurel was dealing with the disorder because the jobs she wanted required working with people at least part of the time.

"How did it make you feel going inside the bank?"

She knew what her therapist wanted to hear. "I sat in my car for a while and told myself I could do it. I needed to do it. I have things I want to do, and I'm tired of disappointing myself." She paused and took a fortifying breath. "I deliberately exhaled evenly. I counted to fifty. Those actions worked down the apprehension, and I got out."

Dr. Easton encouraged her with a nod.

"I'd never been inside the bank before so I looked around, grounded myself. A young woman at a desk right inside greeted me, and I went to the counter and completed my transaction. When the teller spoke to me, I replied. Something about how cold it had been the night before."

"And how did you feel when you got back to your car?"

Laurel recalled the intense relief of having gotten through that experience. "I didn't feel terrible. I can't help the overwhelming sensation that something is going to happen. Something bad. In my head I rationalize it, and I know I'm going to be all right, but the dread is there anyway."

"But you didn't get that feeling inside the bank?"

"I started to…but I reminded myself I want to get better, and I walked to the teller window."

"That's really good, Laurel."

"Oh, and I waved to the mail carrier five times." Pathetic how she knew that. "Twice there were packages that didn't fit into the box and he brought them to the door. I thanked him." She flipped to the back of her planner where she'd written the list and studied her notes.

'Socialization builds confidence. Exercise one: Talk to the person who delivers mail. Engage the check-out girl. Converse with the bank tellers.'

She'd written down these encounters as though she might forget. She was nothing if not thorough.

"You did well. I'm going to give you the entire list, but you're only going to move to the next step when you're confident with the current one."

Confident might be a stretch. She crossed her ankles and sat a little straighter. "How many exercises are there?"

"Six. There's no rush to get through them. No pressure. Take your time."

"I've had time. I've had years." Recognizing her frustration, she stopped and looked at her hands holding the cup. "I went to college and got two degrees. A couple of the classes were online, but not most of them. I've gone to interviews, and I've even worked in a couple of offices." Laurel lifted her gaze back to Dr. Easton with a shrug. "But then something happens and I'm right back where I started. I've been doing this for too long."

"You're not back where you started now. You've come a long way. Temporary setbacks aren't failures. You want to improve, and you are improving. There's no scale to determine what's normal and what's not. Our goal is healthy."

"But I see others who behave normally, and I know I don't."

"You can't compare yourself—."

"But I do."

"Others haven't had the same experiences, Laurel. You've done counseling with other survivors. Did that help?"

Laurel nodded. "I wouldn't even be here if it hadn't helped."

"I see these exercises as reviewing the steps and growth you've already made." She handed Laurel the sheet of paper. Laurel read it over.

Socialization builds confidence.

Exercise #1: Talk to the person who delivers mail, the check-out girl, the bank tellers.

Check.

Exercise #2: Join a group or take a class/lessons.

In person? Okay, this isn't so bad.

Exercise #3: Make eye contact through 60-70% of a conversation.

Holy crap.

Exercise #4: Change your automatic reply from "no" to "yes" thereby opening growth potential. "Would you like to get a cup of coffee?"

Holy crap.

. . .

Exercise #5: Rather than only listening and asking questions, share something about yourself. Respond by linking your own experiences and knowledge.

Call an ambulance. I'm having a heart attack.

Exercise #6: Focus on the present, not the intimidating what-if possibilities.

Right now, in the present, I'm going to screw this up.

Exercise #7: Express emotions/fears out loud. Put negative emotions into words and thereby lessen that emotion's intensity.

"I can't do this."

She'd said that out loud.

She looked up at Dr. Easton, who wore her reassuring smile. "You put feelings into words with me."

"Because that's how therapy works."

The doctor tilted her head. "Yes, it is. But you have all the other steps to work through until you get to that one. You understand what you're working toward and how cognitive behavioral therapy challenges you."

Laurel nodded. "I'm challenging mistaken beliefs by confronting them."

"Yes. Avoiding challenges—or people—won't make you happier in the long run. I didn't show you all the steps to intimidate you, but to prepare you."

Laurel sipped her coffee. "My contentment is not dependent upon external forces or events, but upon me," she recited. She could do this. She would do this. "Okay."

"After you've spoken to a few more people and are

comfortable with that, I want you to move on to exercise two."

"All right."

Her counselor nodded. "Good. You're doing well." She closed the folder on her desk. "Laurel, can you see a time in the near future when you might share your story with someone?"

A collage of disjointed images battered her senses, and she knew enough to let them wash over her in a wave and settle back into the ocean of her buried experiences.

"My story isn't something someone brings up while making idle small talk with the bank teller or the mailman." She took an even breath and thought a moment, imagining a future possibility. "If there's ever someone I feel safe with, a friend or something, I might be able to tell them."

"It's good you were able to let yourself see that." She gave Laurel an encouraging nod. "What are your plans for the rest of the day?"

Laurel worked remotely on three part-time jobs, earning enough to pay the rent on the lake house. She'd been thinking of another project though. "How much do you know about the history of Spencer?"

"I've been here twelve years, and I have a few friends who were born and raised here, but I don't really know much of the history—well except what I've seen at the Pony Express Station and the restored schoolhouse in Olde Town."

"That information caught my attention, too, and I did some reading about the Aspen Gold Lodge. I was considering researching local history."

"As in for an article or a book?"

"That's not really my thing. But maybe I could put something together for the tourism board to use on their website and sell it to them. Or sell the idea of revamping their website."

"Sounds like a great idea. Are you prepared to talk to people?"

"Librarians and historians are talkers themselves. Once you get them started, you just listen."

Dr. Easton laughed. "Sounds like my job."

"Not at all." Laurel shook her head. "You ask deep questions."

"Okay, no comparison." She pushed back her rolling chair, stood, and got her coat from a rack near the door. "I'll walk you out."

Laurel didn't make eye contact with the doctor's next patient in the waiting room. Her therapist accompanied her outdoors and wished her a good day. Pulling on her gloves, Laurel unlocked her vehicle and got in. She'd go home, collect herself and do a little research before deciding where to start locally.

She liked this tourist town. People in Spencer, Colorado didn't ask many questions. The locals respected that tourists were temporarily escaping their everyday lives. She appeared as a tourist, and the anonymity suited her just fine. Twin Owl Lake was the quietest, most peaceful place she'd ever found. She headed north on Chickering Road East and followed until it became the highway that wound northwest past acres of bristlecone pines, blue spruce and cottonwood trees with leaves now turned to gold in the brisk November weather. She had no idea who her neighbors were, though she'd admired the house with the porch and the red roof. She'd seen several different vehicles parked in the side drive, and had assumed it was another rental.

The interior of the house she rented had been remodeled and was managed by a realty company for the owner, a man named Ben Rumford. Apparently, it had looked more like a cabin at one time, but the interior had been drywalled and painted, the kitchen and bathroom updated, the floors sanded and varnished, and a huge deck built on the back, offering a magnificent view of the lake.

There hadn't been mail delivery yet today, so with a plan in mind, she started a pot of coffee. While it brewed, she made herself a hot cup of tea. Grabbing a sweater, she carried her laptop and an afghan to the back deck and settled on one of the comfortable cushioned chairs. She could lounge out here in the sun forever, stay in this rented cabin and never go out again—if the groceries wouldn't run out. She had made a point not to search for grocery delivery. Okay, she could stay right here if there was FedEx pickup, and if her therapist hadn't assigned six exercises to complete. And of course, if she didn't want to get well.

At the sound of the mail truck winding up the road, she hurried in to the coffeemaker, poured steaming brew into a takeout cup and pressed on the plastic lid. What if the mail carrier didn't drink coffee? What if he liked sugar or cream? She ignored her naysaying insecurities and strode out the front door and followed the stone walkway to the road.

The dusty Jeep slowed and the driver hesitated at the point where he could reach her mailbox. Spotting her, he rolled the vehicle a few feet farther to hand her a few pieces of mail through the open window. "Afternoon, Miss Whitaker."

"Good afternoon." She accepted her mail with one hand and handed him the coffee with the other. "It's not sweetened, but I can go grab sugar if you like."

He raised his steel-gray eyebrows in surprise, but gave a shake of his head. "Nah, I like it black. This is a treat. Thanks. I usually don't get a hot cup until I finish the lake route and stop in Spencer for lunch. This time of day my Thermos has cooled off."

"Maybe you'd have preferred something cold."

"No, this is perfect. Thank you."

She didn't feel any ill effects from talking to this person. He was friendly and had a nice smile. "You're welcome."

"You've been living on the lake here about six months now?"

She nodded. Yes, and in all that time this was their first conversation.

"Name's Reuben," he said. "Reuben Trumbull."

"Laurel." But of course, he knew her name.

He nodded and turned aside, presumably to secure his coffee before looking back.

It was only a conversation if she said something more. "I was just starting to research Spencer online, but since you likely know a lot about the town, maybe you can tell me something."

"If I can, sure. I've lived here my whole life."

"I was wondering where I might start to do research on the town. I'm searching for special interest features."

"Aunt Cora would likely be a good resource for you. Cora Fleming is her name, but everyone calls her Aunt Cora. She wrote a historical book about the area, and she's president of the historical society."

"Where would I find her?"

"Aunt Cora's Attic. It's a home turned into an antique and collectable shop west on Silverville Road. You could find history there and probably at the library. Also, the *Spencer Herald*. There's an extensive records morgue in the basement. It's on the north side of Brook Park next to the VFW."

"That's really helpful. Thank you."

"Any time. Thanks for the coffee. The sky's looking like a storm. I'd better get finished with my route." He drove the little truck north toward the next neighbor.

She glanced at the blue sky and didn't see anything except a few scattered clouds. Back on her deck, now wrapped in her afghan, Laurel googled the places he'd mentioned to search hours of operation. She called the number for Aunt Cora's Attic and got a recording, so left a brief message.

The library closed early three days a week, so she tried the *Herald* and was told she could come any time before eight p.m. They were printing the weekly paper that afternoon.

She became engrossed researching online and lost track of time. To prevent intentionally letting more time slip, she stopped and made herself a sandwich before filling her water bottle, grabbing her charger and her laptop case.

❧

Cale Hartwood, the slender owner of the *Spencer Herald* was in his late thirties, though he had thinning pale hair that he tried to stand up and scrunch to appear like more. When she'd asked to search information in the morgue, he'd turned a suspicious brown gaze on her. "I don't have time to babysit you down there. I'm putting out a paper. Only the last twenty years are online. Everything before that is on film."

"I don't need a babysitter. I only need access to the files. They're public, right? I know how to use a microfiche machine. Just point the way."

"I'll have to unlock the room for you. It's climate-controlled to preserve the film and computers."

"I know how to use a key, too."

If he had more hair, it would have bristled. He pulled a face and looked her up and down as though measuring her trustworthiness. He finally took a key from his pocket and extended it. "Be back up here by nine. I don't want to stay later than that."

She accepted the key. "I will. Thank you."

Laurel flipped up the light switch and yellow illumination lit a set of steep wooden stairs. As she descended, they creaked beneath her weight. The area immediately at the bottom of the steps was clean and smelled of ink and paper like the rest of the building. Tall gray filing cabinets and plastic totes lined the walls of this outer room. She used the key to unlock the metal door leading to another room and pushed it open. Holding her breath, she groped along a brick wall and found the light switch. Thankfully, the overhead lights in here were bright, probably LED.

"This isn't so bad." She dropped the key into the pocket of her coat, glad she'd changed into jeans and her thick-soled boots. The floor was concrete and the temperature cool. The door stayed open on its own, thankfully. She set down her laptop bag and purse.

Several metal cabinets stood against one wall. Wooden worktables held cardboard boxes, an old-version microfiche machine, two desktop computers and a printer. Four well-used rolling office chairs provided adequate seating. Laurel turned on all of the electronics and took out her notes, notepad and laptop. Research fascinated her, so without a goal, she'd be perusing files forever. To prevent getting lost, she referred to the list she'd created earlier after a quick Google search.

She searched for Aspen Gold Lodge first, since the town seemed to have grown up around it. On microfiche she discovered that in the 1850s, a man named William Spencer won the land in a card game and built a stage station. William had one son, Thomas, and over time the waystation attracted other entrepreneurs. With the added businesses, the town of Spencer was born on the banks of the Gold River. Thomas Spencer had two sons; the eldest, Jakob, was still associated with the lodge. She found the younger son David's name in the obituaries. A younger sister, Naomi, was still alive. With a head for business, Jakob had capitalized on the growing popularity of the Colorado mountains as a getaway for wealthy guests.

An old map intrigued Laurel, especially the area around the town square. She was certain she'd spotted an art studio now located where the old mercantile had been. Most of these original buildings were still in use. Thankful for Wi-Fi that reached the basement room, she used her laptop to find an aerial map and compared. She printed copies and would pay for them before she left.

An hour or more later, her stomach rumbled. She should have thought to pack an extra sandwich, but she kept a few granola bars in her bag. Soon drawn into another search, her hunger was forgotten.

"Anyone down here?"

The male voice startled her. She jerked upright on the chair and glanced at the bottom corner of her laptop screen. Ten? How had that much time slipped past? The mistrustful owner had told her to finish up by nine.

"Hello?"

If this was that Hartwood fellow coming to yell at her for keeping him past hours, his voice had changed. "I'm still in here," she called. "Sorry, I lost track of time. I'll lock up."

An unfamiliar broad-shouldered man in a blue and gray jacket and uniform ducked to pass under the top of the doorway and took a few steps forward. Laurel's heart leaped and the already-small room threatened to close in. The man between her and the exit wore a brimmed hat, and his silver badge glinted under the overhead lights. A black equipment belt around his hips held cases with flaps and a holstered gun.

The foreboding sensation that something bad was going to happen sucked the air from her lungs. She inhaled and exhaled evenly, forcing composure. "I—I've been doing research."

He grinned. "That's what folks usually come down here for. Haven't had the pleasure of meeting you before." He took a step closer.

Laurel couldn't jump off the chair fast enough. She

moved back several steps. "Sorry. I'll collect my things and go."

Obviously recognizing her unease, he halted. "No hurry. Hartwood let you in?"

She fumbled in her coat pocket and held up the key. Her fingers trembled ever so slightly. "He gave me the key and told me to finish up by nine. I lost track of time, and I guess he forgot about me."

"That's okay." He nodded. "I'm Sheriff Cavanaugh. Joe. I was on my way home and noticed the lights down here. Not an ordinary occurrence, so thought I'd better come check it out."

"If the place is closed up, how did you get in?"

"The janitor was just leaving, and I asked him to hold the door so I could check out the place." He jabbed a thumb over his shoulder. "I'm not suggesting you have to leave, but the storm is picking up out there."

"There's a storm?" She glanced up at the windows, and indeed flashes of lightning brightened the blackness. She wasn't challenging her mistaken beliefs; she was drowning in them, so she arrested her thoughts to make conversation. "I didn't realize...I didn't even know how late it was." She gestured to the files open on the desktop computer and her stack of notes. "I got lost in what I was doing."

"Easy to do. Are you staying in Spencer?"

She nodded. "Yes. I have a rental on the lake." She gathered her wits and counted to ten. Twenty. What would a normal, not overly-cautious person do? Thirty. "I'm Laurel Whitaker."

"Lodge side or the east side?"

"Excuse me?"

"Lodge rentals are on the northwest end of Twin Owl. Private properties on the east."

"Oh." *Oh?* This was not how normal people conversed,

she was sure of it. "East side. The cabin belongs to a
gentleman named Rumford."

He raised and lowered a hand. He wore a watch with a
wide black leather band. She couldn't see his face well
because of the shadow created by the brim of his hat, and
that increased her discomfort. He was tall, over six feet.
"We're neighbors," he told her.

"What? We are?"

"Yeah," he said with half a chuckle. "My daughter and I
live in an Airstream beside you to the south. I've wondered
who was staying in Ben's place. I've seen your car, but renters
come and go."

"Right."

"You probably couldn't hear the storm down here, could
you?"

She shook her head. "No. I should be going."

"Well, it was nice to meet you, Laurel. Spencer is a safe
place, but if you'd like me to walk you to your car, I'd be—"

An ear-splitting crack and a bright flash of light cut him
off. He turned toward the window, but she shrieked and
backed up against the wall.

"It's okay." He held up his palm toward her. "Probably
only a—"

The overhead lights flickered and went out, plunging
them into darkness.

Laurel's heart rate accelerated. Something bad was actually going to happen. "I have to get out of here."

A loud hum sounded, followed by the creak of hinges and
a solid snick as the door closed.

"Well, hell," the sheriff said into the pitch black. The
reconciled tone of his voice sent a shudder of apprehension
along her spine.

'Focus on the present, not the intimidating what-if possibilities.'
She was nowhere near step five. The present was definitely
intimidating. No amount of counting was going to settle her

nerves at this point. The bad thing was happening now. "Wait. I have a key."

She fumbled in her pocket and came up with the key Cale Hartwood had given her. Groping the tabletop nearby, she found her phone, turned it on and used the light from the screen to make her way to the closed door.

She stared at the door, ran her fingers over the surface, finding nothing. There was nowhere to insert a key. Frantic now, the key made a clink on the concrete floor as she yanked on the safety bar. She tried pushing it. The only portal out of this basement room was securely locked. She silently cursed wave after wave of internal trembling that took over her knees and made her hands quake. Flattening her palms on the cold steel, she gripped it in an attempt to steady the quakes.

"We're locked in."

CHAPTER TWO

*L*aurel's phone light turned off and she thumbed it on again, then found her flashlight icon and turned on a meager beam of light.

"We're locked in," she said again.

"Looks like it. That idiot has this security system rigged to lock everything up tight if the electricity goes out."

"Call someone!"

The sheriff took his phone from a pocket and turned it on. "No signal. I can't figure that out. Were you getting Wi-Fi on your laptop down here?"

"Yes." She hurried to the table and checked her laptop. No bars. "Nothing. There must be some way to contact someone."

"With the power out, I don't know what that would be. Wind and lightning like that could have taken out a cell tower. We're at the base of the Rockies, so signals are blocked from that direction. I checked in my walkie and body cam before I left the shop."

Her heart raced, and she couldn't get enough air in her lungs. Everything was going to be fine. She was going to be fine. These were only symptoms, and she didn't have to fix them. She only had to moderate her reaction to the symptoms. For years, she'd been retraining her brain to handle situations. She could handle this one. There was no other choice.

"I have water." She rushed to her bag.

"We won't be in here long enough to dehydrate."

She unscrewed the cap. "Sipping helps me work through stress."

In the dimness, he removed his hat and set it brim-up on one of the tables. "Okay." He rested a hand on his hip. "But drinking will also make you have to pee."

She stopped mid-sip and screwed the lid back on. Embarrassment eddied up her body to warm her cheeks. "I hadn't thought of that."

He pulled out a rolling chair and seated himself with a creak.

"You could try to break down the door," she suggested.

"That door is solid steel. Those doors withstand fire and criminals. I'm not Superman."

"You're going to just sit there?" Her ire was obvious in her tone and volume, but she didn't have the wherewithal to temper it at this moment.

"Unless you want me to sing or recite the pledge of allegiance or something."

Backing up, she crossed her arms over her waist and grasped her elbows to keep herself from trembling. She counted silently. How long would her phone battery last? "If my phone battery dies, we'll use yours. If that dies, we'll use the laptop."

"For light or playing Candy Crush?"

"For light, of course."

"Okay." Joe was trying to keep the situation optimistic. This young woman was obviously terrified. Afraid of the dark perhaps, adding to that the fact that they were locked in and lacked communication…and she was most likely afraid of him. She'd been uneasy since the moment he'd shown up. He did feel pretty useless, and he wasn't accustomed to feeling like this. It was his job to take charge and help people.

"What about the windows?" she asked.

"See those iron bars? They're about eight inches apart." He hated being the one to veto all of her suggestions, but these were the facts. "If we broke the glass, not even you could get through that space."

"We could yell."

"Police station is four doors to the west. No windows on either side. VFW on the east, and there's nothing going on over there. Church behind us."

"There might be someone out."

"It's storming. There's no traffic on the streets. If there are any people out, they're clear across the park at the Wild Card Saloon. There's music and televisions." He shook his head and shrugged.

"How long do you think it will take for someone to find us?" Her voice was thin and shaky. "Or for the electricity to come on?"

"Will anyone be looking for you?" he asked.

She hugged herself, obviously not wanting to answer, but finally replied, "No."

"Me neither. I'm off the clock. My daughter's at home, but she's fifteen. If there's electricity at the lake, she'll stay up playing on the computer or talking to a friend. Otherwise, she'll go to bed. She's used to me working late or having an emergency call. If she needs anything or is frightened, there are neighbors close. Someone in my family might go check on her. They'll figure I'm working."

"Oh-h." The syllable was barely audible.

It was always best to tell the truth. Sugarcoating bad news wasn't fair and didn't help. In his line of work, he'd given enough bad news to know. "Emergency services will check for downed wires or fires. They'll help the utility company find and repair the problem. How long that takes will depend on what's happened."

No one would look for her. He rolled over that fact. "Hartwood knew you were here, didn't he?"

"He was busy getting a paper out," she replied. "He told me to lock up and then must've forgotten I was down here."

"No one might call and think it's odd that you have no phone service? Family?"

"No," she answered simply.

"Hannah from credit card services?"

"Who?"

"It's a robocall everyone gets. I have no idea what they're trying to sell, because I've never stayed on the line long enough to hear the pitch." He rested one ankle on the other knee and leaned back in the chair. "You don't think I'm funny."

She pushed her hair away from her face and shrugged. "Sorry. I'm coping here."

He couldn't tell now if her hair was black or dark brown, but before the lights had gone out, he thought it had been black. "Claustrophobia?"

"Something like that," she answered.

He gestured to the microfiche machine and the pc. "So, what did you learn from your search?"

As though appreciating his transparent attempt to put her at ease, she moved to the table and picked up a notebook page. The paper trembled, so she laid it down and held the phone over it to see her writing. "I found the origins of Spencer and how in the 1800s a man named William won the land in a card game. He was the great-grandfather of the man who runs the Aspen Gold Lodge."

"That's the story."

"You're related to the Spencers?"

"That I am. My grandmother is Jakob's sister."

"Naomi," she clarified. "Your family has been here a long

time." She unfolded her arms. "Do your folks live here? Siblings? Tell me about them."

"Are you sure? There are a lot of them."

"I'm sure."

"My dad passed away a few years ago. He was a good man, a great dad. My mom is pretty great, too. Amazing, actually. My grandmother on my father's side is still alive. My grandparents on my mother's side have a place here, but they winter in Florida. I have three brothers and two sisters."

"Where do all of them live?"

"Right here. My oldest brother has two kids, teenagers now, and a lovely wife. The brother younger than myself works at the lodge. He has a seven-year old and recently got married. His new wife owns the house on the other side of where you're living."

"The one with the red roof?"

"That one. And my youngest brother, Crosby is a landscaper. He's perpetually unattached, but has a different date every other week. We all get together for dinner on Sundays."

"Dinner every Sunday? At a restaurant?"

"Rarely. No, we still meet at my folks' house. Mom and the others cook. Summers we grill outside."

"You mentioned your daughter. What about your wife?"

"It's only been the two of us since Chloe was a baby."

"Oh. I'm sorry." He hadn't said if he was divorced or widowed, and she didn't ask.

"That's okay." Everyone in Spencer knew his wife had left him and his daughter, so he wasn't used to people asking. "Talking seems to help you stay calm. What other coping techniques help?"

"There are several. Taking slow and deep breaths. Counting. Staying put instead of running." She flapped a hand toward the door. "Check."

"Smart, though. That's so you don't have an accident if

you're driving—or maybe run somewhere less safe than the place you're in. What else?"

"Reminding myself that the frightening thoughts and feelings will pass."

Sounded like a tough call to him. Trauma was immediate, and so were the feelings that went along with it. "So, applying that to this situation, how would you do that?"

"I remind myself that nothing is permanent. Every situation ends eventually." She still paced back and forth, but her voice sounded steadier.

"Right," he said. "Either the electricity will come on or someone will find us. What else?"

"Focus on something non-threatening. Other people. The time passing."

"I got the feeling I'm threatening."

"Yes."

"The uniform? My size? My gender?"

"Yes."

He suspected her anxiety was different from or more than claustrophobia. "You're not having a panic attack, though?"

She shook her head. "It's not like that."

"Does anything else help?"

"Challenging the fear by assuring myself it's not real. Being aware of a problem or my reaction to it doesn't change anything. I have to challenge my reaction."

"I'm not sure I understand that one. Fear seems pretty real. This situation is real." He stopped. "Sorry if that was unhelpful."

"No, you're right. That's a tough one. Fear is fight or flight. Real fear demands action, like when a rattlesnake at your feet raises its head and vibrates its tail—that produces fight-or-flight fear. The danger is concrete and real. When we're concerned that we might say or do the wrong thing in a situation, that's a fear we can work through. Embarrassment doesn't kill anyone."

"I get it."

"Thinking about a positive outcome or imagining positive situations is helpful."

"So, talking now is helping?"

"Yes." She stopped pacing and sat on one of the other chairs. "Thank you, Sheriff Cavanaugh."

"Joe."

She nodded. "Tell me more about your family."

He thought a minute. "My daughter is a dancer. A very talented one." He sat comfortably, his arms crossed over his chest. He was thirsty and getting hungry. He usually ate when he got home. "I had my doubts about dance at first. It was cute when she was little, but then she started talking about studying at academies in New York and planning her future based on which one she could get into. I didn't want to see her have her dreams dashed. Or maybe holding her back was selfish of me, because it's always been the two of us, and studying elsewhere would mean she'd leave home."

"Probably a little of both," Laurel reasoned. She had no idea how it felt to be so attached to someone, but she could imagine it.

Occasionally, she let herself imagine it.

"Probably. But a prestigious dancer started teaching at the community college in the summers, and this past summer Chloe was finally old enough to get into her class. Kendra has toured in big time troupes and danced at the Kennedy Center."

"Wow."

"Yeah. And she helped Chloe get a scholarship in New York. Chloe won't attend until she finishes high school, though."

"That sounds like a wonderful opportunity."

Joe couldn't have agreed more. "Still. Growing pains

aren't limited to the kids. Parents experience them more, I think."

He'd always been a talker, and he liked people, but maybe it was the darkness or their seclusion that encouraged him to feel comfortable with this young woman. He didn't know her, and she wasn't forthcoming with information, but talking obviously calmed her. He'd had this subject on his heart for a while. It wasn't as though the chief could share his insecurities about fatherhood with his poker buddies at the Wild Card.

"Do you have confidence that this instructor has your daughter's best interests at heart? It's unusual in a competitive arena for a performer to give a younger one a leg up."

"Well, Kendra married my brother. They're newlyweds actually. They had a small ceremony at my mom's. It's Kendra's house there on the other side of you. Her focus has changed, and now she's doing choreography. I do have confidence in her. We've talked a lot."

She was quiet a long moment. "Your family really is close."

Her earlier comment had him assuming she might be comparing her opposite situation to his. He attempted to revise the subject. "So, you're researching Spencer or the lodge...are you a journalist? Travel magazine writers and bloggers come through fairly often."

"No," she answered. "I'm a social media manager. I build websites and create social media presence for companies. I do write, though, and sometimes I sell pieces to online zines. I'm putting together a package for the local tourism board, and I'll find other uses for what I find as well. This area is rich in history and flavor, so there's likely treasure to be found."

They talked about the historical buildings in town and he told her how the old schoolhouse had been restored and moved to Olde Town. He explained how the Old Stone

Church was still in its original form and that now artists occupied the interior with workspaces and sales areas. "There's a Pony Express Station with a museum too."

"Spencer has a fascinating history. I'm intrigued." Laurel picked his brain about the community and stories he remembered about the old timers.

Much later, Joe checked his watch to discover a couple of hours had passed. "I suppose it's time to open that water bottle."

"I have another one." She reached into her bag and pulled out a plastic bottle which she handed to him. "Oh, and I have granola bars. Sorry, I forgot about eating. You must be starving."

She handed him two wrapped narrow bars and kept one for herself.

"I don't need two," he objected.

"Yeah, you do. Your body weight is probably twice mine." She visibly cringed. "That's not a bad thing—I didn't mean—you're not…."

He laughed. "I get it. I'm bigger than you. Thank you. I'm missing my mom's leftover beef and noodles sitting in my fridge."

"Stop it." She unwrapped her granola bar. "I'm visualizing a positive outcome right now." She closed her eyes. "I'm eating a big fat burger, and there are fries on the side."

"A beer," he added.

"Okay," she agreed without disrupting her muse by opening her eyes. "They're sweet potato fries."

His stomach growled. "You must be eating at the diner in Olde Town. They have the best burgers." He ate his first granola bar slowly. "I'm appreciative, but reality is missing something. Like the beef."

She actually laughed, and he liked the sound.

They finished their meager meal and each took a couple sips of water.

Laurel stifled a yawn.

Joe got to his feet and turned on his phone flashlight. He inspected the boxes and other items in the room. "Shame someone doesn't use this place for secret trysts or an occasional nap. At least there would be a cot or a mattress."

"Come to think of it, this would be a great storm shelter," she added. "Except there's no way out."

"There's probably a safety device on the door that stops it from locking if the person down here is prepared for a storm and sets it," Joe thought aloud.

"Might have been nice to know," she added.

"But you're right. This cellar could be used as a storm shelter." He opened a few creaky doors on the old metal cabinets. In the last two he tried, he discovered quilted moving pads, a case of water, and several pop-top cans of spaghetti and ravioli. "Bingo."

"What?" She hurried up behind him.

He turned and handed her a can.

"We have supper after all," she said.

He appraised the can he held. "I haven't eaten one of these since I was a kid."

"We don't have forks or spoons," she pointed out.

Joe took his pen from the black holder on his belt and held it up. "But we have skewers."

"Right." She went for her pen. "I will not think about how unsanitary this is or that there's ink on the tip of the pen."

"Or that it's too dark to see the expiration dates."

"I did not hear that."

They sat and ate their canned pasta.

"This isn't that bad," she said.

He wiped his pen off on a piece of paper. "Are you going to have to...you know, go?"

Laurel groaned. "I'm not miserable yet, but yes."

"There was a carton of coffee mugs in one of those drawers."

She mumbled something under her breath.

"What?" he asked.

"Okay." She got up. "Which drawer?"

After answering, he got up and, with a screech of metal on the concrete, moved one of the filing cabinets away from the wall. With his phone lit, he checked behind for spiders. "There you go. Privacy."

She carried a mug bearing what he assumed was a *Spencer Herald* logo behind the filing cabinet. "Make some noise out there."

He pulled up the meager selection of music stored on his phone, which wasn't much because he listened on an app that required Wi-Fi. He tapped the first song. A slow beat filled the silence before female voices joined it. *'Walking down the road and watching as the sun goes down; Heading to the place I go when I've got stuff on my mind; No one's there, no one's around....'*

"I haven't heard this," she said. "Who is singing?"

"Seeker Lover Keeper. Chloe and I found it for a dance routine."

He turned up the volume.

When she returned, he handed her his phone before taking care of business. "Keep the music going."

A few minutes later, he pulled out the moving pads and unfolded them. "These are pretty thick. We can probably make ourselves pallets. Better than the cold concrete anyhow, and I'm beat."

Laurel took two of the quilted pads he extended, folded both in half lengthwise for more thickness, and made herself a place to lie down. The sheriff was trying his best to put her at ease, and she appreciated his efforts. "I'm going to keep my phone light on as long as I can."

He was good with whatever made her feel safer. "Okay."

She took off her coat long enough to remove her cardigan and handed it to Joe. "For a pillow. I'll use my bag."

Joe removed the equipment belt that held his gun, rolled
it around the weapon, opened a file drawer and placed it
inside. "I'd never get any rest with all that bulk around my
hips. You okay with my gun in there?"

She shrugged back into her coat. "I guess so."

The next song played with a throaty female voice singing,
*'If you ever lose your way, and everything is out of place, I'll be
there to make it all okay,'* followed by hauntingly sweet, *'Ohh
ohh ohhs.'* He let it play until the end. He thought the music
might have calmed her, but he needed to save his phone. "I'm
turning it off to save the battery."

"It's okay."

It was so quiet he could hear her breathing. Under his
head, her sweater held the fresh scent of something herbal,
like maybe her soap or shampoo. The feminine scent was
disturbing and yet innocently enticing. He made himself
think about tomorrow's paperwork and the list of wellness
calls he had to make before the weather became severe.

After about forty-five minutes of lying in silence and
hearing her every move, he asked, "Are you cold?"

"Yes."

"We could lie closer for body heat."

"I don't know if I can do that."

"Okay," he said easily. "I don't want you to be uncomfortable."

He shifted his hips. The pads weren't enough to cushion
his weight from the concrete.

A few minutes later, she said, "All right. If we get closer,
we can double the padding underneath us. Maybe use one as
a cover."

"Okay." He helped her make the adjustments to their
pallet. They knelt and faced each other. "Want me to lie
behind you, or do you want to be behind me?"

"I'll lay behind you," she answered.

He laid down and faced away from her.

She stretched out behind him, her body along the back of his, and pulled a moving pad over both of them. "This is better," she said.

He agreed. "I think I'm comfortable enough to sleep now."

Laurel lay listening to his breathing and recognized when it grew deep and even. What she wouldn't give to know the peace this man possessed. He was a county sheriff, so he'd seen and done a lot. This was probably one of the least difficult challenges he'd faced—or else he simply took everything in stride like a normal person.

What did that feel like? What did it feel like to encounter a frightening new experience and face it without his body or mind betraying him? It must be wonderful. Did normal people notice when they were being normal?

Shut off your mind, Laurel. Just *be* for the love of all that is sacred. Stop analyzing, stop imagining worse scenarios... just stop.

They'd be out of here in the morning. There was no possibility of starvation in that amount of time. The worst had already happened. She'd freaked out in front of the sheriff. She'd peed in a coffee mug in his presence, for crying out loud. She hadn't even had a good look at his face, so he hadn't seen hers that well either.

How would she ever face him in the daylight?

She shivered. His body heat seeped through her clothing, however, so she flattened herself more closely, tucked her knees behind his, which placed her cheek between his shoulder blades. His jacket held a vaguely woodsy scent with a hint of cedar. She relaxed against him. The trembling of her limbs stopped. Tomorrow if it wasn't freezing cold, she would sit on the back deck that overlooked the calm waters of Twin Owl Lake and the blue expanse of sky and enjoy the open space. She might even go for a burger.

A loud buzz and the glare of the overhead lights startled Laurel from sleep, and she bolted upright.

Beside her, the sheriff sat and blinked against the brightness.

Oh, my goodness. His wavy dark hair was charmingly disheveled. He ran his fingers through the mass, taming it only minimally. His sleepy eyes were the deepest darkest brown, with flecks of gold around the irises. He had a straight nose, lips with a deep top divot, and his square jaw wore a dark shadow of a beard. A tiny scar on his chin grew no whiskers.

He was surveying her every bit as intently, but caught himself and pushed to his feet. He picked up her wrinkled cardigan and handed it to her.

Laurel quickly finger-combed her hair, stood and hurried to the door. She picked up the key she'd dropped the night before, shoved the safety bar and the door opened. The yellowish light above the stairway was on as well. Relief flooded over her in a wave, and she wanted nothing more than to charge up those stairs, out of this building and escape into the daylight. Instead, she stood in the outer room and looked back into the paper morgue. Her things were in there —her purse, her laptop. Her heart rate increased uncomfortably, so she inhaled a deep breath and released it slowly.

The lawman appeared in the doorway opening, his weapon once again belted to his hip. He held her laptop case and purse. "It's all here. I checked and got everything."

Laurel nearly fainted at the realization that she was liberated from that room, and her reaction shamed her. He'd done his best to put her at ease last night, made every effort to calm her, assure her, lessen her embarrassment. She'd slept with her cheek against Sheriff Cavanaugh's wide back, his body keeping her warm. She stared at him, with his rumpled uniform, bulky jacket and finger-combed hair, and counted to ten. Twenty. "Thank you. For everything."

"You're welcome." He carried her bags forward and handed them over, then went back for his hat and held it as he followed her up the stairs.

Laurel finally had the presence of mind to check her phone. It wasn't six yet. She glanced around the front of the office and opened a gate in the balustrade that separated the office from the visitors' area. Inside a room off to the side sat a huge antique printing press. The walls outside that room were hung with framed front pages of the *Herald* and enlarged black and white photos of men in aprons running the presses.

"Tourists can print their own headlines on mock issues on that old press," Joe Cavanaugh said from behind her.

She placed the key she'd been given on a front desk. "Will we be able to let ourselves out?" she asked.

"We should be able to open the front door and have it lock behind us," he answered. "If not, I'll handle it."

The door opened for him, and he gestured her out ahead.

She stepped outside and inhaled the cold pine-scented air. The sky was clear now, but the sidewalks and street were littered with leaves and debris. Across the street, several limbs were down in Brook Park. She glanced at the evergreens blanketing the foothills and mountainsides to the north.

"The door's not locking behind us," Joe said. He pulled out his phone and touched the screen. "Phone's working." He tapped a contact. "Morning, Jericho. You in the shop? Will you come keep an eye on the front door of the *Herald* until I can get Hartwood over here? There was a little mishap and the front door is unlocked. Yeah. All good. Thanks." He set the phone in his belt. "My deputy will be right here. That your Toyota?"

Her metallic gray RAV4 sat beside a black crew cab pickup. "Yes."

She kept her remote on a clip inside her bag, so she unlocked the doors.

The officer followed her, and she glanced back, surprised to notice he was limping slightly as he approached her car. His silver-star badge reflected the light, 'Rockwell County Sheriff's Department' in blue letters forming an outer circle around an aspen leaf design in the center. She opened her car door and got in. He rested his forearm on top of the door. The early morning sun burnished his hair with a mahogany tint. His disheveled hair and day's growth of beard softened the intensity of his size.

There was a little mishap...' He'd taken the whole event in stride and even done his best to put her at ease. Self-disappointment was a rock in her gut.

"I'm sure we'll be seeing each other, since we're neighbors," he said.

"Probably." She glanced aside and then up at him. "Thank you. For everything. I feel bad that you got locked in because you came to check on me."

He raised a palm. "Don't give it another thought. I consider it a good night if I don't have to chase anybody through pitch-dark backyards or put someone in jail." He dropped his arm. She gave more attention to his grin and the creases in his whiskered cheek than she should have. "I'll grab a shower and a fresh uniform and be good for the day."

He stepped back.

She offered a smile.

He settled his hat on his head.

She turned the ignition, started her vehicle and eased out of the space onto the street. After putting the transmission into drive, she checked her rearview mirror.

The sheriff was getting into his truck.

Laurel went over Dr. Easton's list in her head. Did this count for anything? Could it be called socializing if they'd been trapped together? They had talked...well he had talked more than she had, about his family, his daughter. Their phone lighting had been too poor for eye contact to count. She had looked directly into his eyes this morning, however.

And then probably stuttered or something, because she'd been getting a real view of him after their forced intimacy.

She hadn't shared anything about herself. That point always bothered her, because that was something she would never do. She couldn't lie, but she wouldn't tell the truth. As soon as someone even suspected she was hiding something or asked too many questions, she'd be out of here. Moving on as she always had.

She hoped it didn't happen at all. She liked living on the fringes in this tourist town, and she'd made a lot of progress with Dr. Easton. Friends were not an option.

CHAPTER THREE

$\mathcal{L}$ aurel had a protein shake, showered and napped for an hour, and it was still morning. Regrettably, the sheriff probably didn't have the same opportunity. Or perhaps, since he'd been working last evening, he worked a later shift today.

Catching herself giving too much thought to the man, she got out her laptop bag and sorted through her notes and the copies she'd made. She'd have to go back and pay for them. She doubted she'd be able to go down into that morgue at the *Herald* in person again, but she had plenty of jumping off places for Internet searches. And she still hadn't spoken with Aunt Cora, the woman the mailman had mentioned.

After an hour or so, she got out her journal and wrote about the previous night. She flipped back through the pages and read the to-do list she'd copied from Dr. Easton's typed version. She supposed it was time to move on to the second exercise.

She'd promised herself a burger the night before, but instead she made herself a turkey wrap, pulled on her coat and took her lunch out to the back deck, where the sun warmed the cushions on the cedar furniture.

'Join a group, take a class or lessons.'

Pulling up the Spencer community college on her laptop, she scrolled the class offerings. Welding was a skill she probably wouldn't use soon. Green living sounded interesting. She dismissed cast iron cooking, glass etching, ballroom dance, and water aerobics. Self-defense for women caught her interest. *'Learn how to logically thwart and evade an attacker. Dynamic training in simple and effective techniques. Certified instructor.'*

Living isolated as she was out here, knowing how to protect herself could come in handy. She'd meet other women with the same goal. A class full of women who wanted to protect themselves didn't sound threatening. Laurel scrolled the page, found the enrollment section, an available time slot, then registered and paid.

She was checking her receipt when her phone rang. She usually let it go to voice mail, but feeling empowered, she answered. "Strategy Blitz, this is Laurel Whitaker."

"Ms. Whitaker," returned the unfamiliar male voice. "This is Jakob Spencer calling from The Aspen Gold Lodge. I understand you're living nearby."

Jakob Spencer? The sheriff's great uncle? The man who owned and oversaw one of the most lucrative and security-tight hotels in the nation? Her hand trembled holding the phone. "Yes—yes, I'm living on the lake actually. How can I help you, Mr. Spencer?"

She was getting cold, so she carried everything inside and locked the glass door.

"I was wondering if you could work an appointment into your schedule. My staff tells me we're behind the times with all of this social media business, and one of them is married to a teller who met you at the bank. We're looking to bring ourselves up-to-date, so I found your website. Do you think you can help us?"

Apparently, speaking to people had more benefits than

she'd imagined. Laurel worked to keep her voice even and not squeal into the man's ear. She set her open laptop on the kitchen table. "I can definitely help you. Do you have anyone doing your social media right now?"

"My executive secretary. We had our accounts designed and set up a while back, and her foster kids used to help her, but she's overloaded and doesn't have time to learn more. She thought reservations was handling social media, and they thought someone else was. It is not a typical mix-up, I assure you. I pride myself in running a tight ship."

Laurel typed the Aspen Gold Lodge into her browser and checked the first listings. "It's a lot to learn if you're not technically savvy. I'm looking at your portals right now. You're definitely due for some updates, and your listings should be the first to come up in a Google search. They're not. Do you have a PR staff? Advertising? It would be helpful if they were included in the meeting. Seeing your advertising and marketing efforts would help me too."

"You're interested then?"

"I'm interested, Mr. Spencer." She went to the glass door and glanced across the expanse of the lake. All the property on the other side, from the shore to the foothills for acres and acres belonged to this man and his multi-million-dollar corporation. The fact that he'd called her personally attested to his down-to-earth approachability and that of this mountain community.

"Wonderful. I'll put you through to Andrea Paulson now, and she will work with you and the others you mentioned to coordinate a time. I look forward to meeting you."

"Thank you for the opportunity."

"I like to work with the locals whenever possible," he replied. "And I had you checked out. You're worthy of the task."

A spasm of unease had her standing straighter. Of course, he'd had her checked out. The lodge catered to some of the wealthiest and most influential people in the world. She'd be willing to guess they'd done a thorough background check before considering her. The familiar sense of unease washed over her and receded. Her background check had passed their security. The court had securely sealed records of her identity many years ago. "I appreciate your confidence."

"Hold on now." The line clicked and almost immediately a female voice greeted her.

Several minutes later, arrangements made, Laurel studied the lodge's social media outlets, opened a new file, and added notes. Her Spencer project could wait for now. This was the biggest opportunity of her career. Within the hour, she'd lost herself in research and ideas. She would have a presentation to wow Jakob Spencer and his marketing team when she showed up at the lodge next week.

⚜

Two days later, she was putting together her PowerPoint presentation, with all of her work on the dining room table when there was a loud rap at the front door.

Startled out of her reverie, she straightened and looked out the window to discover the mail truck. Laurel pulled open the door.

"Hello, Mr. Trumble."

"Call me Reuben. Say, I have a package for your neighbors next door to the south. Would you mind if I left it with you? There's no one home. If I'm not able to leave it with a neighbor, I have to haul it back, check it in, and bring it back tomorrow."

"Sure. Not a problem."

"Great. I'll leave a notice in their box so they know that the package is over here." He turned, lifted a small carton from the porch floor, and handed it to her. "Thank you. You enjoy the rest of this beautiful day now."

"I will, thanks." Laurel carried the package with the familiar logo into the house and set it on a chair beside the dining table, curiously glancing at the address label and feeling oddly vindicated that Joe Cavanaugh shopped online. It wasn't only introverts avoiding people who ordered from the mega online seller. Now she'd be talking to him again. Dr. Easton would like that.

From time to time on weekends, she'd heard truck engines, saws and hammers echoing nearby, but the thick trees and brush prevented her from seeing anything other than an occasional glimpse of light at night. He'd mentioned he and his daughter lived in an Airstream. She'd Googled it and learned it was an RV, and not a cheap one, depending on how big and how new.

She figured he or his daughter would see the note in their box and come for the package, but quickly immersed herself in her work and forgot about it. By six she was hungry, but she'd forgotten about food too, so she took a frozen chicken breast from the freezer and set it on the counter. She'd fix it with a salad later. The box on the chair repeatedly drew her attention, so she freshened her face and hair and picked it up.

Wearing her boots and coat, she set out for the Cavanaughs. She could have driven, but she often walked along the road for exercise anyway. Lately, she'd been considering getting a dog for company. It might be nice to have a companion on her walks, as well as during the day and at night. A pet was something she'd never given thought to before. Pets were for stable people who stayed in one place. The lake cabin was a rental, but she had the option of a longer lease. There was a rescue shelter somewhere near Spencer. She'd check it out sometime.

The trees had lost nearly all of their glorious gold and red leaves, but the bristlecone pines with their dark green were a year-round contrast. The scenery was beautiful here. She'd never lived anywhere with such an expanse of sky and abundance of lush color. No wonder the town and the lakes drew tourists. Google searches had revealed there were any number of things to do, such as trail rides, go carts, mountain biking, camping, fishing, shopping in historic Olde Town, great food, drinks and dancing. Once she'd initiated herself into her self-defense class, she would try out a few of those activities.

She neared a mailbox and spotted 'CAVANAUGH' painted on the side in neat black letters. Not a big enough mailbox for someone who regularly ordered from the largest online retailer though. She'd had hers replaced with one large enough to hold serious packages. She quickened her pace along the gravel drive.

In the waning sunlight, silver gleamed through the foliage. Laurel came upon an Airstream, apparently a permanent dwelling, evidenced by the red-and-white striped canopy, assortment of lawn furniture, nearby grill and even a couple of half-barrels overflowing with yellow chrysanthemums that had seen better days. A black Chevy Tahoe sat nearby under the protection of enormous trees—the truck that had been parked beside her vehicle outside the *Herald*. Her stomach dipped nervously. Was he home? Would she see him again?

A young girl in a puffy pink coat sat on a picnic table, one finger scrolling across the screen of her phone. At Laurel's approach she glanced up and raised her eyebrows. "Hey."

"Hi." Laurel used her thumb to indicate the direction from which she'd come. "I'm your neighbor. The mail carrier left this today."

The teenager got up. "Sick. I hope it's my Otter Box."

"For your phone or iPad?"

"iPad Air. I ordered pink with lime green."

"When I first checked into moving out here to the lake, I was skeptical. My first question was to ask how good the Wi-Fi was, and the realtor assured me it was excellent."

The girl nodded. "The tourists spend a lot on the rental cabins, so everything up here's high tech."

"I'm Laurel Whitaker."

"Chloe Cavanaugh. My dad and I live here." She pointed to the Airstream with a roll of her eyes. "My dad's building a big cabin over there, but it's taking a really long time."

The door to the mobile home opened, and the sheriff stepped out carrying a tray. He wore his uniform, dark trousers and gray shirt with official patches sewn on the upper part of the sleeves. His cuffs were rolled back, revealing corded forearms. No gun on his hip.

The flutter in her stomach wasn't her usual wash of nerves, but still a warning. Awkwardness never killed anyone, she reminded herself.

He spotted her. "Hi, Laurel. I thought my daughter was on the phone. I didn't realize we had company."

She took a deep even breath. "I walked over with a package. The mail carrier left it with me."

"Thanks." His star-shaped silver badge gleamed in a waning shaft of light that speared through the autumn-sparse canopy of cottonwoods. But she was taking steps to overcome anxiety, so she took a deep breath and counted to ten. The unease receded.

"You two know each other?" Chloe asked.

"We met in town," Joe answered simply.

'Exercise number three: Make eye contact.'

Laurel got a fluttery feeling in her chest, but she raised her chin and looked into the sheriff's gold-flecked brown eyes. "It was no problem to bring it over. I like to go out for a walk anyway."

He set the tray holding steaks and grilling tongs on the picnic table and gave her a smile that created creases in both cheeks. Definitely disturbing. "This stretch of highway is pretty year 'round, but it always seems bleak after the leaves have fallen."

"When I rented next door, the realtor told me all the land on this side of the lake had been in families for generations. He said owners rarely sell because it's a steady income. Was this land in your family?"

"No. Ben Rumford and my granddad were fishing buddies. Ben's father had a cabin on that land where the house you're in is now, and he owned this lot as well. My dad used to bring me and my brothers here to fish and stay overnight. Back then there was no electricity or running water."

"What did you *do?*" Chloe asked as though he'd faced the end of the world.

He glanced at his daughter. "We caught fish during the day. Cooked our meals over a fire. Enjoyed nature."

"*Bo*-oring."

He cast Laurel a grin. "Kids. They think they have to be wired to the Internet all the time."

His lashes were enviously thick and black. Holding his gaze made her stomach dip, but she held on so she could tell Dr. Easton of her progress. Plus, gazing into his eyes wasn't so bad.

"When Ben moved to the care center, he kept that portion of the property as an income and sold this section. I was fortunate to have grown up friends with him, and he offered it to me. He knew how much I loved this place."

"That was fortunate," she agreed.

"Sorry," he said. "Did you two meet? Laurel, this is my daughter, Chloe. Chloe, this is Miss Whitaker. She's a... what's your job title?"

"I'm a social media consultant. Wired to the Internet all the time."

He didn't flicker even one of those thick black eyelashes.

She lowered her gaze to the Rockwell County Sheriff's Department emblem on his badge.

"Why don't you stay for supper?" he asked. "There's an

extra steak. I'll throw them on and you can watch them while I go in and change."

"Oh, no, I—" *'Change your automatic reply from no to yes, thereby opening growth potential.'* That was step four. She wasn't ready for step four.

"You're staying. We're neighbors, and we should have gotten better acquainted before now." He turned to pick up the tray, opened the lid of the grill, and used the tongs to place the meat on the grates. "Chloe, entertain our guest for a few minutes. I'll be right back. Then we'll go inside where it's warm and eat."

Chloe had gone back to her phone, but she laid it on the nearest small outdoor table. "Would you like a cup of coffee? Or a beer? Dad has beer too."

He hadn't given her time to modify her automatic reply from no to yes. He'd decided for her. Did that even count? No, it didn't. She wiped her palms on her jeans. "I'd love coffee, thanks."

Laurel lifted the lid of the grill and peered at the slabs of beef. She had no idea how to grill a steak, but these looked especially good. She'd been eating chicken and salads because she knew how to prepare them.

Chloe returned and handed her a hot mug.

"Thanks." She glanced at the Airstream. "How long have you and your dad been living here?"

"We used to come out on the weekends, but then last Spring my dad decided we shouldn't be paying for a house in town when we have a perfectly good tin can sitting here that we can squeeze into. So, we sold the house and here we are."

"The two of you?"

"Yep. I never had a mom. Well, I had one, but I never knew her. She left when I was a baby."

"I'm sorry."

"Yeah. Me too. What about you? Do you have family?"

"No. It's only me."

Chloe turned to the shipping package on the picnic table and peeled tape from the carton. "Don't you love online shopping?"

"Actually, I do."

Laurel turned over the steaks, hoping she wasn't doing this wrong. The cooking beef made her mouth water.

The door to the Airstream opened and Joe came out wearing a pair of worn jeans and a T-shirt with cartoon dogs playing cards at a table. She recognized Scooby Do, Odie, Snoopy and Pluto. He noticed her regard and touched the image with a palm. "It was a gift from the guys at the Wild Card. We play poker on Tuesday nights, and they thought this was funny."

"It is kind of funny."

"He only wears it when we need to do laundry," Chloe added.

He shrugged. "How do the steaks look?"

"I turned them over. They smell great."

He picked up the tongs and opened the grill cover.

A rustling in the nearby brush startled Laurel, and when a large dog bolted out of the timber and ran toward them, she jumped.

The yellow lab ran directly to her.

"Stay down," Joe commanded.

The dog didn't jump up, but sniffed her shoes and the legs of her jeans.

"That's Barney. Good boy, Barney."

The dog moved to sit before Joe.

"You smelled the meat on the grill, didn't you? You be a good boy. Lay down, and you'll get a bone later."

The animal looked away, then moseyed across the grass, sniffing here and there.

"I've never heard him."

"He doesn't bark much. Once in a while old Jonas Finch's dog barks from over north, and Barney barks back." He rested the tongs on the wooden rack at the end of his grill. "The steaks are almost ready. Chloe, will you make the salad please? I'll be right there."

"I'll help," Laurel said immediately, hoping her offer didn't sound as though she was trying to escape being left outside with him.

"Come on." Chloe gestured for Laurel to follow her inside.

The door led into a kitchen and eating area with padded benches on either side of a table to the right of the entrance and the sink and appliances to the left. The kitchen opened to a surprisingly large living area with a sofa and chairs. They hung their coats. Chloe got plates from a cabinet and handed them to Laurel. Next, she gathered forks and knives and together they set the table and made a salad.

Chloe glanced at her. "So, you know all about what? Social media?"

"Yep. And websites. I help businesses develop a presence and show them strategies for maintaining, based on their goal and needs."

Chloe grabbed her iPad from the counter and unlocked it with her pin number. "What's the name of your business?"

"Strategy Blitz with a Z."

"I like that."

"There's no picture of you. Who's this guy in your profile pic?"

"A stock photo."

"But you're beautiful. You should have your photo there."

The compliment caught her off guard. "Thank you, but it's not about me. It's about providing a professional service."

"So, could you help me find more friends? Cool friends?"

"Probably. But you would have to outline why you want them and what you will do with them once they're following you."

"Well, maybe I just want to know some cute boys." She

met Laurel's eyes. "That's not what you do, huh? Hook people up?"

"No. I find ways to hook up businesses with customers."

"But you could give me some tips, right?"

"Number one. Anyone you meet online could be a predator. Check them out and be suspicious of everyone."

"You sound like my dad."

Laurel took a sip of her coffee. "Your dad is smart."

"What is it I'm smart about?" Joe climbed the few stairs carrying a tray of aromatic steaks. He set it down.

Chloe removed Styrofoam packing from the box she'd set aside to reveal her case. "I love the color." She figured out how to get the Otter Box cover into place. "I can drop this baby from a roof now, and it will be safe."

Laurel nodded. "Very cool." She tipped her head toward Chloe. "Probably not from a roof, though."

"Obviously, our ideas of safety differ," Joe commented. He took a seat at the table and gestured for Laurel to sit while Chloe got bowls.

She felt awkward sitting across from him. She counted under her breath and said in a low tone, "You can set parental controls."

"That sounds like what it is," he answered. "Controlling. She already has her phone. I laid out the rules, and I want to trust her."

"Do you?"

He nodded. "She's a good kid. She has goals and dreams for being a dancer, and I don't believe she'd do anything to hurt those plans. She's a teenager now. Without a mom. I'm doing the best I know how. But she has my mom, her aunt Colette, and her new aunt, Kendra."

"The dancer."

He nodded. "Kendra worked hard to achieve her success. She's a good role model."

Laurel was curious about Joe's family, but especially the new sister-in-law he thought so highly of.

Chloe served three pretty salads with spring mix lettuce, cherry tomatoes and cucumber slices. "The dressing's already on it," she said and scooted in beside her dad.

Laurel couldn't remember the last time she'd eaten with someone. It had been years. Occasionally, she sat in a café or restaurant, but more often she drove through for take-out or cooked something easy for herself. Meals had been a solitary event for her, even during her youth when she'd been forced to sit in the cafeteria with the other students gawking at her as though she was a lab specimen. Back then, she'd pretended she was alone, so she could get through the ordeal.

Laurel looked at the bowl in front of her and emotion rose up in her throat. If she had a comfort zone, this would be the polar opposite. Her vision blurred. She counted to ten. Twenty.

"It's not fancy," the sheriff said. "Chloe and I eat pretty simple food, and our nice dishes are packed."

Thirty. Laurel picked up the fork, but she couldn't look at either of them. He'd sounded apologetic. Laurel found her voice. "This is nice. Really nice. I'm not used to anyone asking me to dinner."

Their silence made her wonder if she sounded like a freak. She collected herself. What would a normal person do? Laurel glanced up. She smiled at Chloe, and then let herself peek at Joe. The sheriff. "It's all perfectly lovely. Thank you."

The awkward moment passed, and they started their meal. She cut into her streak and tasted the first bite. The flavor exploded on her tongue. She chewed and enjoyed. "What kind of steak is this?"

He glanced up from his plate. "A T-bone. See the shape of the bone? It's T-shaped."

"Oh. Yes, of course. I don't know if I can eat all of this."

"You can take your leftovers home for tomorrow."

She nodded. "Yes. Thanks."

His daughter glanced at him, but Joe continued to eat. Their guest's behavior was a little odd, but he understood she was working on things, and he didn't want to embarrass her. Thankfully, Chloe was a perfect hostess. It was unusual for them to have anyone join them for supper. Their surroundings were sparse for the time being, but they got by. They always went to his mother's for Sunday dinner and occasionally during the week. He was used to family and friends, laughter, and people talking over each other.

Laurel Whitaker was an enigma. She was strikingly beautiful, with shiny near-black hair, dark wide eyes and pale luminous skin, but he suspected she placed little store in her physical appearance. She mostly avoided eye contact and often appeared as though she'd rather disappear than have any attention drawn her way.

But she lived alone and had goals for her career, which he admired. She was obviously independent and self-sufficient. She'd been terrified of him when he'd shown up in the newspaper morgue the night of the storm. More afraid of him than of the storm—and then completely unnerved by being locked in. Anyone would have been, but he suspected the incident was something more with her—something to do with fear of closed spaces, probably more than that. She lived and worked within what she saw as the safe environment of the Internet, websites and social media, where there was no personal face-to-face interaction.

Talking to people, eating dinner with them was apparently so far outside her comfort zone that she was using her coping mechanisms to deal with something as simple as supper with the neighbors. He'd guessed how to count along with her, mentally noting high and low stress levels by the length of time she counted.

When he'd asked, she'd said she had no one. No family? Didn't everyone have some family somewhere? She'd deliberately been evasive, which made him more curious. It was in his nature to figure out people, understand their motivations. He'd meant to look up anxiety disorders to have a better understanding.

"Where are you from, Laurel?" Chloe asked a little later. She'd finished eating and hadn't picked up her phone. His daughter was intrigued too.

Laurel patted her napkin to her lips and took a sip of her coffee, likely cold by now, maybe collecting her thoughts, planning her reply. "I was in Arizona before coming to Colorado. The Phoenix area."

"Must be different than here," Chloe said. "Cactus and sand and stuff like that."

"Very different. Have you been there?"

Chloe shook her head. "No. Dad and I went to California once. That was fun. And we went to Washington. I went to Minneapolis with my Grandma and aunt and cousins once. Grandma and Aunt Colette drove."

"That's quite a road trip."

"It was great. My dad made me call him every night. He missed me."

Laurel had skillfully deviated the subject from herself back to Chloe. Joe looked over at his daughter. It had been the two of them since she was an infant. Being a single parent wasn't for sissies. "It was way too quiet in that house."

He met Laurel's eyes, and she smiled a soft smile that tipped up her lovely mouth at the corners. It was quiet at her house every day and night, too, but some people liked it that way. She wasn't forthcoming with her thoughts, which intrigued him.

It wasn't his business to know everything about her, but he was curious—and maybe suspicious by nature. It went along with the job. Their neighbor was hiding something.

CHAPTER FOUR

*C*hloe transferred the remainder of her steak to his plate, and he finished it. He had Chloe slip out of the booth, so he could get to the door. He opened it, called Barney over, and gave him the bone. The three of them watched together out the bank of windows, with curtains wide open showing the panoramic vista of their property, to see the dog cart the bone over to the tree line. He settled in the brown grass to chew.

Chloe slid open a window. "You're a spoiled dog, Barney," she called.

The yellow lab looked up, licked his chops, and went back to his treat.

Joe and Chloe chuckled. "It's a good thing we're going to live out here," Chloe said, shutting the window. "I don't think he could go back to living in town and staying in his yard."

"He likes the woods," Joe agreed.

"Can you imagine all the smells out there?" his daughter asked with a grin. "Raccoons and squirrels and deer. He's in dog heaven."

Joe looked up to find Laurel observing them. "Are you full?"

"Stuffed. I've never had a better steak."

"Dad saved a guy's life years ago, and the guy still sends him Omaha Steaks a couple of times a year."

Laurel's eyes widened with interest. "You did? How did you save his life?"

He shrugged, "Just doing my job."

"The man and his wife slid off one of the mountain roads in the snow. The wife was thrown from the car, but the man was trapped inside."

"That must have been terrifying. Was the wife all right?"

"Banged up, but she was okay," Joe answered.

"My dad tied himself to a tree trunk and climbed down the side of the mountain to get the man out. He got the man up to the road and then the car went the rest of the way down the mountain."

"Oh, my goodness. Do you have climbing gear?" she asked.

He nodded. "We live in the mountains, so there are plenty of rescues."

"You truly did save his life," Laurel said in awe.

"Anyone trained to help would have done the same," Joe told her, embarrassed at her look of admiration. "I just happened to be there."

"Thank God for that," she said. "No wonder the man sends you steaks."

"Dad shares them with the deputies, too," Chloe told her.

"Okay, that's enough stories." He got up and picked up their plates, stacking Laurel's on top. "I'll put your leftover in a bag."

With water running in the sink to mask her whisper, Chloe said, "He gets all embarrassed about that stuff. He's received commendations from the commissioner for acts of bravery, and he puts 'em away in a drawer. Most of my dance trophies are packed away right now until the house is finished, but once we move in, they're coming out. I like to see them. They remind me of my event competitions and how hard I worked. I'm not embarrassed about that."

"Everyone's different," Laurel said.

"Do you have anything like awards or diplomas?"

"I have diplomas for my degrees."

"Are they on your walls?"

"No." Laurel shook her head. She placed the salad bowls and silverware in a stack. "Can I help wash dishes?"

"Nah. That's my job."

Joe laid a bag with her steak on the table. "Don't forget that. Would you like a fresh cup of coffee?"

"Oh, you know…it was so kind of you both to share your meal with me. I enjoyed it very much. Since Chloe won't let me help with the dishes, I'd better get going. You two enjoy the rest of your evening."

"It's getting dark earlier," Joe said. "I'll walk you to your place."

"No. No, I'm fine, really. Thank you."

"Thanks for bringing over the package," Chloe said.

"Not a problem. Good night now."

Joe grabbed their coats and held out hers so she could slip her arms inside. He put on his as they stepped out of the Airstream. "I'll walk with you part of the way at least."

She managed to turn her head and look at him. He met her gaze and her stomach dipped. "This really is the best steak I've ever had. Actually, I didn't know steaks tasted this good. I'll enjoy the rest of it tomorrow."

He nodded. "Glad you liked it."

Silence stretched between them as they walked. Did he and Chloe think she was odd? Did they suspect she wasn't forthcoming about her past? She'd behaved as normally as she'd known how. She'd eaten a meal with them, talked to them, listened to their stories. Fascinating stories, really. Stories of normal people with normal lives. She wondered what that felt like.

She'd done research on rational emotive therapy, and learned that what people need most in the early days of their recovery is the support of family and friends, a resource she'd never had. Therapists couldn't allow personal relationships to develop, so while she'd grown comfortable with them and appreciated their help and direction, she'd never known complete acceptance. But the ability to allow people close was the problem.

Well, part of the problem.

This man had no idea what a big deal it had been for her to come inside his home and sit at his table. Apparently, he had a big laughing happy family. She had the uncomfortable feeling that he could see right through to her flaws. It was obvious she didn't fit in. Anywhere.

"Thanks again," she said when she spotted her cabin and realized he'd walked her nearly all the way. "Supper was really nice."

She sprinted ahead of him and ran toward her rental home, feeling foolish, but feeling relieved once she reached the porch, unlocked the door and stumbled inside.

❧

"You're welcome." She hadn't heard him. She'd bolted as though a pack of wolves was on her heels.

Laurel was a puzzle, an intriguing beautiful, dark-haired, feminine puzzle. He should let it go, not think about her or about the questions that rolled through his mind. A light came on inside the cabin. He imagined what she'd be doing this evening, wondered how it felt to be all alone and comfortable with her solitude. He was the second of three brothers, and two sisters had been adopted after them. Life and noise had always surrounded him, so much so that he and Chloe seemed incomplete without the others.

But people were different. He accepted that. He saw it

every day. She didn't need fixing, and even if she did, fixing her wasn't his job.

Barney met him on the road and trotted alongside back to their property, where the dog promptly took off across the underbrush.

"You'd better come back before dark if you want to sleep inside," Joe called.

He opened the Airstream door and climbed the stairs.

Chloe was putting away the last of the dishes. He wrapped his arms around her slender form and hugged her. "You're a good daughter, Chloe."

She hugged him back. "Thanks, Dad. You're not so bad yourself."

He chuckled and released her.

"Laurel's pretty cool, isn't she?"

"Is she?"

"Yeah." She hung up the dish towel and turned. "She said she didn't have any family. How can that be?"

"I don't know. Some people don't have big families like we do. She might have had older parents who have passed away or something."

"That would suck. Or maybe she has horrible parents like Aunt Kendra, so she doesn't have anything to do with them."

"Aunt Kendra has made some peace with her mother, but maybe it's something like that. Everyone is different."

"We could invite Laurel for Thanksgiving."

Joe turned from hanging up his coat to look at his daughter. Of course, she would think of that. She was as used to crowded homes and holidays filled with people as he was. Chloe adored her cousins and aunts and uncles and grandmother. "You can ask Grandma if it's okay."

Chloe picked up her phone. "You know she'll say yes."

"But Laurel might not say yes, and we have to respect her wishes."

"It'll be okay, Dad." She texted his mother.

❧

Laurel showed her identification to the blue-uniformed security guard at the front gate of Aspen Gold Lodge. He checked a tablet and apparently found her name. With a friendly smile, he handed her a trifold map of the grounds. "Good morning, Miss Whitaker. Welcome to Aspen Gold Lodge. I'll let the staff know you're here."

She thanked him as the wide scrolled iron gates automatically opened before her, and she drove onto the property. Ahead was a sprawling white five-story hotel with a red tile roof. Long covered porches provided the second floor with balconies. Massive windows on the lower level were shaped in graceful curved arches, and the top floor windows were set into peaked dormers. The structure was even more impressive in person than in the photos and brochures.

Laurel wasn't sure where to park, so she pulled under the portico, thinking she'd have a few minutes to get the layout in her head, but another staff member in blue trousers and a coat with a gold emblem came to the driver's door.

She rolled down the window.

"Good morning, Miss Whitaker. I'll park your car for you. Do you have anything you need help carrying?"

"Oh. No. Only my bag here." She picked up her computer bag and purse and got out of the car, leaving it running.

"If you want to dial 012 on a house phone when you're ready to leave, I'll have your vehicle waiting."

"Thank you." So much for time to gather herself. She stood in place as he got into her vehicle, took deep breaths of the cold mountain air and counted. Turning, she climbed wide stone stairs to the top, where one of the wide polished double doors opened and another staff member in gold dress shirt and blue trousers ushered her inside.

"Miss Whitaker?"

"Yes."

"Hi, I'm Clark. I'll escort you to the meeting room where Mr. Spencer is waiting for you. May I take your bag?"

She nodded, somewhat dazed by the carved wood arches, pillars and chandeliers in the lobby, and handed him her computer bag. Over to her right was a wide expanse arranged with tastefully elegant conversation areas on thick rugs with standing potted plants for privacy.

Clark bypassed a grand sweeping staircase leading to a mezzanine above and led her to the elevators. Inside the first one, he pushed the mezzanine button.

She counted to twenty.

The doors swished open silently.

"Right this way."

She followed him, daring to look over the railing at the elegant lobby below, the sparkling chandeliers above, hoping he didn't notice her awe. Her helper paused outside a doorway and gestured for her to enter ahead of him.

"Mr. Spencer, Miss Whitaker is here."

A tall, slender white-haired gentleman in an impeccable dark gray suit turned from the windows and walked forward to extend his hand. "Miss Whitaker. It's a pleasure to meet you. Thank you for agreeing to this meeting."

"Of course," she managed, placing her hand in his warm one. His intense green eyes surprised her, but his genuine smile wrinkled the corners of his eyes and deepened creases in his cheeks, putting her at ease.

"Clark will take your coat. There is hot tea, a coffee machine and pastries on the sideboard over there. Please help yourself. The others will arrive in a few minutes. I wanted some time to talk alone before they got here."

She relinquished her coat to the helpful young man and noticed then that he'd placed her computer bag on the long table near the head.

She was delighted to find a single brew coffeemaker and a salted caramel pod in a rack, so she brewed a familiar and delicious-smelling cup of coffee. The aroma helped to settle her nerves. She was prepared and a pro at her profession. She knew instinctively this old gent was a shark, but he seemed genuinely kind—and he'd sought her out.

She added milk and carried her mug to the table.

"Do you need your computer hooked up to the overhead screen, Miss Whitaker?" Clark asked. "I can do that for you."

"Yes, thank you." She got out her laptop and he handed her a cord.

Jakob had seated himself at the head of the table next to her. "Two college degrees and a nice resume of past employment are impressive credentials. I checked your references for the businesses and websites you've worked with and looked at their financials. Every one of them saw an increase in profits after your overhaul."

This man obviously had a lot of contacts and some serious investigators working for him. She had suspected as much. "That's good to know."

"I like to get to know the people who work for me."

"That must be quite a list."

"It is. But I think that's what keeps Aspen Gold running so smoothly. Everyone knows what to expect. We respect each other's positions and time, even the down time. That's important."

"That's unusual for an operation as large as the lodge," she said. She checked the connection, opened PowerPoint, and her first slide came up on the overhead. She thanked Clark.

"I like to think we're unusual. We are professionals with a lot of responsibilities, but we are also people with busy lives and families. There was a time I worked so much, I neglected my family, and that lack of balance caused problems. I hope I've changed. I hope my children and grandchildren think I've changed."

Laurel didn't know how to respond. She sipped her coffee. "You have a big family from what I understand."

"That I do."

"I've met your nephew, Sheriff Cavanaugh."

"Under pleasant circumstances, I hope. He didn't write you a ticket or anything."

She laughed. "No ticket. But the circumstances weren't what I'd call pleasant. We were trapped in the basement morgue at the *Herald* the night of the storm. I was researching. He saw lights on and came by to check. The electricity went out and the door shut."

"I did hear something about that, but I didn't realize it was you. You'd think Hartwood had a vault of gold bullion down there, rather than dusty stacks of old newspapers."

"It's quite clean actually. And most of the data is on computers or microfiche."

"Double check anything you find printed in the *Herald* in the last ten years," he told her. "The man bends the facts."

"I'll remember that, but I'm really only interested in the origins. Spencer itself is the gold mine, rich in history and potential."

"I'm eager to hear your proposal," he said finally. "Do you have anything you want to discuss before I buzz in the others?"

She appreciated his thoughtfulness, but also wondered about his purpose. She had the feeling he was waiting for her to tell him something she didn't want to tell anyone else, and that made her uncomfortable. There was no way his security team's background check had discovered anything she didn't want them to know, but fear had been her relentless enemy for so many years, breaking those initial reactions was a work in progress.

She gestured to her laptop. "I have a presentation prepared, so I'm ready when you are."

"Clark, will you tell the others to come in, please?"

"Yes, sir." The young man exited the room.

A few minutes later, two men and two women entered

the meeting room. Jakob introduced them, starting with a lovely, sixtyish Black woman with short graying hair. "Andrea Paulson, my executive assistant and right hand."

"A pleasure," Laurel said and shook the woman's hand.

"Andrea's husband Paul is in charge of gate security. They've been lodge family for many years." Jakob turned. "Deke Ward here is head of security." Trim and fit, Deke was in his forties with mostly gray hair and a neatly-trimmed white beard. "Obviously, Deke has a say in all public information."

"Miss Whitaker," he said with a curt nod.

After the marketing and public relations managers, Jakob introduced the final young man. Laurel had already given him a second glance, noting familiarities she hadn't yet figured out. "This is Dusty Cavanaugh, our operations manager."

"Welcome to Spencer," Dusty said.

"Dusty is the sheriff's brother," Jakob explained.

"I noticed the resemblance," she said, inwardly shuffling information and remembering this was the brother recently married to the dancer.

The newcomers made cups of coffee and took seats, and finally it was time for Laurel to go through the material she'd prepared. "I'm excited about this opportunity to show you the ideas I have for Aspen Gold Lodge's social media and Internet exposure. To share a little about me, I've been creating social media and website content for companies for the last six years. I typically report directly to the founder or CEO, but plan with a team in six-month engagements that require deep strategizing of how to optimize content, track user traffic, analyze user responses, and then using this information, expand the demographic profile."

She smiled and deliberately made eye contact with each person. "In case I'm speaking Greek to anyone, I'll take a few minutes to explain exactly what this means and show you the intended results." She clicked past her credentials and resume to the plan she had for an updated and efficient website. "The Aspen Gold Lodge is elegant, exclusive, featuring amenities equal to the most sophisticated and well-designed hotels in the world. Comfort, privacy and safety are the lodge's utmost concerns, am I correct?"

"You're correct," Jakob replied. "Political figures, Hollywood icons and Olympians have been our guests over the years."

"An extensive background check is done on every employee," Deke told her. "I am adamant about changing routines. Security guards dressed as other staff walk the grounds and check inside and out. There are motion detectors and cameras."

Laurel nodded. "I suggest a slogan something like, 'luxury, privacy and safety, leave it to us.' We can play with that and come up with something you like, but a phrase that cuts right to the lodge's mission and what a guest can expect from their stay. Part of the charm of Aspen Gold is the history and old-world charm, but you want to appeal to a new clientele as well, and an updated, interactive website will help you do that."

She clicked through her ideas for pages and different social media strategies, explaining her ideas. "People love to share their own experiences, and you can provide places for them to do that, which then are free recommendations for potential guests." She glanced at the others' interested expressions. She had them hooked.

"And pets," she continued. "Pets are big business. Sixty-seven percent of US households own a dog, many more than one, and a lot of those people shop and travel with their dogs. You have a childcare facility, but what if there was a pet care facility? A pet spa, where guests could leave their dog while they go horseback riding or mountain climbing? I realize this is stepping out of the social media arena and into your business model, but what I do is stimulate ideas for growth, and I see that as a potential area."

An hour and fifteen minutes later, she signed a contract, shook hands with Jakob and tucked a check into her purse. Excitement teemed inside her, but rather than squealing and jumping up and down, she kept a cool, professional façade. Clark called to have her vehicle waiting downstairs.

Jakob walked along the mezzanine with her. "I knew there was something special about you," he said. "I might be a little set in my ways, but I have a knack for finding innovative people. I'm glad you're on board, and I look forward to introducing you to more members of the staff and to my family. Andrea will call to set up a strategy meeting next week."

Her vehicle was waiting and running, so she thanked the valet, set her bag and purse inside, and got in. Her exultation rose as she drove away from the lodge with a broad smile. Once through the gates, she pulled over on the side of the road, put the car in park, and pounded on the steering wheel, the unexpected rush of excitement too much to contain. She took the check from her purse and stared at it. This was the pinnacle of success she'd worked for, more than she could have hoped for. She'd pitched the biggest job of her life to people who held her fate in their hands. Her voice hadn't quavered. She hadn't missed a beat. Engaging with others had always been easier when it was school or business and not personal or social, but this had been exceptionally rewarding.

She could easily deposit this check from her phone right now, but she was going to park at the bank and go in. She was banking the biggest advance she'd ever landed, and she owed this progress to years of therapy and her investment in the steps.

Yet, a tiny voice in the back of her mind nagged at her, chipping away at her moment of jubilation. What would a normal person do? Absently, she noticed snow on the mountain peaks in the distance.

A normal person would have someone to tell. They'd call a friend or a parent or a sibling and shout their excitement, because moments like this were meant to be shared.

The hollow feeling those thoughts resurrected temporarily dampened her excitement. She put the vehicle in drive and focused on the road. She had the drive back to Spencer to talk down the annoying voice and assure herself this moment was all hers and that she deserved to enjoy it.

She'd be okay. Better than okay.

Back in town, she drove to the bank and went inside. She greeted the young woman at the desk inside the door, signed her check at the counter and deposited it, tucking spending cash into her wallet.

"Have a nice afternoon, Miss Whitaker," the woman said.

"Thank you. That's a lovely scarf," she added.

The dark-haired woman smiled and touched the colorful scarf at her throat with the tips of her fingers. "Thank you. My sister gave it to me for my birthday. She always selects the perfect gift."

"She obviously does." Laurel turned and headed out. That's what normal people did. They conversed. They smiled.

They had sisters who gave them gifts.

Stop, just stop now.

She'd been promising herself she'd go check out Olde Town after hearing so much about it—and she'd promised herself a burger, so she drove east and, instead of taking the highway home, which was her comfort move, she pulled into the area with charming shops, historic buildings, museums and places to eat.

A parking area was easy to locate, and passing it she spotted a magnificent stone church building. The sign read Old Stone Church Artists' Cooperative. Intrigued, she parked

and walked to the beautiful old building. This was what the
sheriff had mentioned. Closer, she found a flip-up box like
realtors used in yards, opened it and took out a colorful
brochure that opened into a map of the area. The old church
was featured.

'Spencer's original fine art cooperative gallery, part
of Spencer's historic Olde Town since 1995. Artist-members
work in all media and operate and staff the ACG. Everything
in the gallery is changed at the beginning of each month with
a special rotating display in the featured exhibit area where
we highlight new & experimental work.
    Hours 9am – 9pm.
    First Friday celebrations 7pm - 9pm.
    Always free. Always accessible.'

The structure appeared to have two levels, a basement, and
three stories on a corner tower area. Circular shapes in the
leaded glass windows added unusual interest. Laurel climbed
the stairs and pulled open an enormous red-painted door.
    She entered into a carpeted lobby with walls lined by
enormous glass display cases and made her way along the
cases. The cabinets held displays of items that had been part
of the original church, like hymnals, photographs, paintings
and candlesticks. Placards described the history. A few other
people viewed the displays as well.
    Other cabinets featured paintings, pots and jewelry. One
held information about Willa Samuels, the woman who had
purchased this building and raised funds to pay taxes, reno-
vate the interior, and establish the cooperative gallery. The
Spencer Historical Society had helped find these original
items. Laurel studied Ms. Samuels' three paintings, done in
bright colors and depicting scenes of the Rocky Mountains,

majestic trees and a shimmering lake. It was obvious the artist loved her surroundings, and it showed in her art.

Stringed music played as a soft background to the visitor's experience. In a pass-through into an area being prepared as a store was a round wood table holding a four-foot flower arrangement and a guest book. The table also held business cards in holders, folders and brochures. She picked up a couple.

Upon entering the enormous former sanctuary with a high wood-beamed ceiling, more visitors milled about the divided areas, half of which were still under construction and separated by yellow caution tape. The finished rooms had been tastefully divided and could be closed off and locked with folding scrollwork gates. Only a few were inaccessible.

The wide center held pews and high-backed padded wood chairs in seating arrangements with a middle display area, apparently the featured exhibit.

Laurel browsed the rest of the building, finding artisans like weavers and pottery makers working in many of the rooms. She watched a woman plop a blob of clay on a spinning pottery wheel, scoop water on it and shape it into a jar in minutes. The woman continually wet her hands, thinning the walls, creating height and then ballooning out the sides with her hands. Last, she put an indented lip on it.

"This is where the lid will sit," she said, glancing up at Laurel.

Laurel hadn't even known the woman was aware of her, so she was surprised to be addressed. She deliberately met the potter's eyes and smiled. "It's fascinating. How do you make the lid to fit?"

"I'll trim the opening and lid, and I'll add a design tomorrow after the pieces are dry. I've done so many, though, I can pretty much guess it will fit."

Laurel stayed and watched her make a lid with a flattened

knob in only a couple of minutes. She severed it from the wheel with something like dental floss and set both pieces on a table of drying jars, all nearly identical.

"They're my bestselling items," the woman explained. "People think of all kinds of things they plan to keep in them. I have a featured display next month. That's why I'm making so many ahead." She cut another piece of clay. "My partner and I teach classes on Monday nights if you ever want to come by and try your hand at it. Pick up one of my cards by the door. I'm Muffy."

"Laurel." She took a business card and tucked it in her purse. "I might like to try your class. Thanks."

She had a lot to tell Dr. Easton, and as she made her way out of the stone building, she imagined sharing everything that had happened this week. She took the map from her pocket and walked a block, contemplating getting a late lunch at one of the restaurants.

Instead she stood outside a place called The Olde Time Soda Shoppe, doubt creeping into her thinking. Looking in through the front windows, she observed two families seated at large tables as well as couples and pairs of friends sitting in the upholstered booths. She'd watched television and seen movies, of course, and she'd observed those scenes with friends having lunch together and discussing their love lives or their jobs or parents. Those depictions only served to make her question if those fictional relationships were put on or if they existed in real life.

By college, she'd taken the name she used now. Most of the publicity about her had died down, so she hadn't been the freak she was in junior high or high school, but she'd deliberately kept to herself and lived off campus, no sorority, no group of friends.

Today she should have had someone to celebrate with her, someone to at least call. How pathetic was it that she was looking forward to telling her therapist her news?

A brisk wind caught her hair and chilled her. This wasn't productive thinking, and she didn't feel sorry for herself. She was a capable and strong woman, confident enough to stride into this establishment and have lunch without needing someone at her side. Besides, people only made her uncomfortable, and this was her celebration day.

Laurel pushed open the door and entered the warmth. She had a date with a hamburger and sweet potato fries.

CHAPTER FIVE

*L*aurel's first self-defense class was scheduled for a few nights later. She'd read the information on the community college website and watched a few YouTube videos, so she'd ordered a long-sleeved black track-suit. She donned it over a t-shirt, laced up her comfortable sneakers, used her GPS and found the correct building.

A dozen women of all ages showed up for the class, and Laurel hadn't needed to worry about her attire. The others wore everything from sweats to shorts and yoga pants. The class was held in a large room with a tiled floor and a couple of enormous padded mats. Signs indicated the restrooms.

"Have you done this before?" the ponytailed blonde beside her asked.

"No. First time," Laurel replied.

"Me too." She wore a pink t-shirt with the words BE KIND across the front with black yoga pants. "I know the instructor, and I have customers who've taken the class. They all recommended it."

Friendly people always made her uncomfortable, but she tamped down her discomfort. "Customers?"

"I work at Pearl's Café, so I talk to a lot of people every day." She stuck out a hand. "Piper Newport."

"Oh." Laurel shook her hand. "Laurel Whitaker. You know the instructor?"

"Everyone in Spencer knows him. He's the chief of the sheriff's department."

The chief?

"Okay," a female voice called over the buzz of conversation. "If I could get everyone to join me and check in, we'll make sure we're all here and get started."

Laurel and the friendly blonde moved forward and gave their names to the middle-aged brunette with a clipboard. She wore a tracksuit similar to Laurel's in a burgundy shade.

One figure loomed over the others, and Laurel immediately recognized Joe Cavanaugh. The chief apparently. "Are we all accounted for?" he asked.

He wore slim black pants and a gray t-shirt that emphasized his muscled chest and arms. The RCSD insignia in the upper left corner of his chest was secondary to his physique, which the other ladies noticed as well, as noted by their smiles and glances at each another.

"Everyone's here, Chief," the woman helping said.

"Remember it's Joe when we're not at work," he told her and grinned. He glanced over the students. "I'm your instructor, Joe Cavanaugh, and this is Deputy Lucas, otherwise known as Vida while we're here. I see a lot of familiar faces." He spotted Laurel and his eyebrows raised, but he composed his expression. "Let's do quick introductions."

In turn each woman gave her first name, and then Joe rubbed his hands together. "If you want to sit on the mats over here, I'm going to go over this training course with you before we get to the physical stuff."

The students seated themselves on the mats.

"Awareness is your best defense. I plan to drill into you the importance of being aware of your surroundings. I'm going to teach you the five principals of self-defense, and number one is awareness. It's a common thing after someone has been attacked for us to hear people say, 'If I had only known.' Well, people don't normally take time to learn how criminals operate or the methods they use to steal or rape or kidnap. I'm being real here. I taught these same principals to my daughter when she was seven years old. I've seen all the bad stuff, and I wanted her to be able to protect herself."

So, Chloe knew self-defense. Laurel was proud of the girl she'd only met once, and she admired this father for teaching her invaluable lessons.

"You don't know when you might find yourself in a dangerous situation," Joe continued. "You need to be aware all the time. While you're driving, buying groceries, walking your dog, at your job or even at home, preparation and awareness are the most important factors in staying safe. It doesn't matter if it's a false alarm, and most of the time it is, but if you see or hear something unusual, immediately assess the situation.

"Running away is better than fighting. Screaming your head off and scaring the person away is better than fighting. A potential assailant knows what he is planning to do, but he's not planning on what *you're* going to do. What I'm going to teach you is how to reduce this person's chances of surprising you and catching you off guard.

"Now, you might have noticed we're not giving you helmets or boxing gloves. This isn't a martial arts class. The only person here who will wear protective gear will be me and Vida because we plan to get the crap kicked out of us. If an attacker came at you in the grocery store parking lot, you wouldn't be wearing protective gear, so training you in gear would be a disservice to you. You'll be holding a purse, probably a couple bags of groceries, and thinking about what you're cooking for dinner when you get home.

"We're going to teach you to scream and kick and use

everything at your disposal to defend yourself. This is going to get down and dirty."

He looked at each person. "Some women's training can lead to false confidence. You're not as strong as a man. Don't throw rocks at me for pointing that out. It's a fact of physical size and weight, so unless you're Becky Lynch, the WWE's superstar, the odds are stacked against you."

A couple of the young women chuckled, apparently knowing who he was referring to.

"Age, physical conditions, and a lot of factors go into your ability to defend yourself. So, because of that, we're going to apply strategies to adaptive circumstances in settings where you might need this preparation. Now, of course we can't cover it all, and it's not my intent to scare you." He nodded to Vida. "I have a couple of videos we're going to watch. And then Vida and I will demonstrate how the women in each scenario protected themselves from being victims."

The first video showed a woman carrying groceries and being startled. She turned around, and the attacker put both hands on her throat.

Joe paused the play. "First, drop whatever you're holding. Crossbody purses are safer than those big bags you ladies love. Whatever is in your purse isn't as valuable as your life. You can replace credit cards and cash. Drop it all. It takes six seconds for someone to choke you unconscious," he said. "He gets his thumbs on those arteries, you're out, and he's free to drag or tow you away."

Beside her, Piper gave a barely audible gasp. Six seconds gave Laurel pause for thought too.

Joe noted their reactions. "I know that's a scary thought, but you're going to learn how to prevent that and break free. Vida, show them an alligator neck. That's what we say when we're teaching the kids."

"It's your double, triple chin," Vida told them, and tucked her head back to made her chin and neck look thick.

"See there, how her neck is shortened and thickened, making those arteries less vulnerable?" Joe indicated Vida should face him. He grabbed at her throat and she thickened her neck. "Now Vida's first instinct will be to try to pull away my hands, but my arm strength is greater than hers, so who's going to win the struggle?"

"You are," the women chorused.

"Even bringing her hands up from underneath and chopping at my arms isn't enough to deter me. Vida's goal is to break free, to scream and run to safety." He turned to his deputy. "I'm really going to grab you this time, so show them how to break free."

Laurel watched breathlessly.

Joe grabbed the much-smaller woman around the neck, his thumbs at her throat. In a quick move, Vida bent at the waist, leaning all the way down, then ducked to the side and broke free under his arm. She let out a blood-curdling scream and ran the opposite direction.

Laurel got chills down her bare arms.

"All her energy was focused on bending straight down, so my thumbs could not stop her body from going straight down. She leaned low enough and then to the side so her head didn't get stuck on my forearm where I could have grabbed her again." He showed the remainder of that scene of attack where the technique was shown. "Now stand up. We're going to break into pairs and practice this move."

Fifteen minutes later, they watched another video. In this one the attacker grabbed his intended victim from the rear in a choke hold. Joe paused the video. "This is a more common approach. The attacker catches the person unaware. Come here, Vida." He stood behind her and wrapped his arm around her neck. "Now, what is her natural instinct?"

Vida grabbed his forearm with both hands, but to no avail. She hung on, and the sheriff actually lifted her more than a foot off the ground and backed away, carrying her. "Now he can easily drag or haul her into isolation."

Several women did a quick intake of breath and a couple murmured.

He released Vida and both resumed their original places.

"We'll demonstrate for you how to break away from this hold. It can be done, even if you're a little bitty thing. Probably even more easily if you're a little bitty thing."

The instructors showed how if a woman put her left foot back, her right foot forward and twisted toward him, jammed her head against him and pushed against his body with both hands, she was able to free herself. "Freeing your shoulder is the key to loosening the predator's hold on you. If he has you in his right arm, you loosen your right shoulder and vice versa."

Joe showed the rest of the demonstration video, and then they practiced. After a couple of partners, Laurel was paired with him.

"Are you stalking me, Miss Whitaker?"

"Your name wasn't on the class description, so I had no idea you were the instructor."

"I was teasing. A couple of us take turns teaching this class, so there's no instructor named."

"Okay."

"You really don't think I'm amusing."

Uncertain how to respond, she shrugged.

"Okay, let's practice." He indicated she should turn away from him. He stepped behind her and locked his arm around her neck. Her heart rate accelerated. If she was confused in this safe setting, simply because a man she barely knew but found disturbingly interesting was uncomfortably close, how would she ever react favorably in a real situation?

Determinedly, she grasped his arm beneath her neck, finding his flesh warm and muscular. She put her right foot forward, her left foot back, and twisted down with her head into his body and broke free.

"Perfect," he told her. "Do it again." She repeated the move a couple more times, and then he said, "This time I'm going to hang on more tightly. Are you ready?"

"I'm ready." She turned her back on him.

As soon as he grabbed her around the neck, she took the steps, struggled to twist, but bent away from him.

"Excellent," he said, then turned to the class. "Great job tonight, ladies. Next time, we're going to get more physical. Tonight, you learned how to get away from a couple of holds, how screaming and running is effective. Hopefully, you'll never need to use these tools, but if you do, these lessons will prepare you. There might come a time when you'd need to physically fight off an attacker, and we're going to show you how—even though you're smaller, even though you might not have the superior strength, you can disable the person long enough to get away. Have a great evening."

Laurel grabbed her bag and headed for the door.

"Are you a local? I don't think we've met."

She turned to a fortyish woman with extremely red hair. "No, I'm renting a lake house for a while. I'm Laurel."

"I usually end up meeting everyone who has a pet, and I haven't met you before."

Laurel shook her head. "I don't have a pet."

The woman laughed. "I'm Emily Daniels. I work at All Creatures Veterinary Clinic."

Laurel smiled. "Nice to meet you." They walked outdoors, and Laurel tugged her coat collar more tightly around her neck. "I have been thinking about getting a dog. The place where I live is a little secluded, so I thought a dog might be nice."

"Which house are you renting?"

"Ben Rumford's."

"So, you're neighbors with the sheriff. Have you met that adorable daughter of his?"

"Yes, I have," she answered with a smile.

"Shame Joe never married again. All these years since his wife ran off, and he never gave that little girl a new mama. I guess she has plenty of women in her life, what with Liz and Colette and those sisters of Joe's. Chloe has grown into a nice young lady."

"I really don't know her well. She's friendly and seems smart and capable." This was the first Laurel had heard that Joe's wife had run off, and she wasn't sure what that meant exactly.

"Truth be told, he's probably better off without that Shelby Long, and so is his daughter. She was a piece of work."

Laurel had nothing to say about that. "It was nice to meet you. I'll see you in a couple of days."

"You too, hon. 'Night." Emily headed for the parking lot.

Laurel got out her remote and walked toward her car. This was a small community, and the residents obviously knew each other's business. She wasn't entirely comfortable knowing Joe Cavanaugh's business, though. The knowledge, even though it was likely old news in this town, felt intrusive. She was the last person to infringe on another's privacy.

On the drive home, she couldn't help thinking about the different environments in which she'd encountered the sheriff. First as a lawman still doing his duty after his shift had ended by checking up on the newspaper building. He'd immediately been sensitive to her discomfort, and when they'd been locked in the dark together, he had distracted her, spoken encouragingly, done his best to ease her distress and discomfort. Next, she'd seen him in his home environment, competently prepping a meal and inviting her to dinner. He and his daughter were obviously close and part of an extended loving family. Tonight, she'd observed the instructor, concerned about the safety of the women in his community and doing something about it.

Why would any woman run out on a man like that?

&

The next evening before he reached home, Joe pulled into the Rumford driveway and rang Laurel's doorbell. While he waited, he turned and glanced toward his property, but even though winter approached, he couldn't make out anything through the dense foliage and trees.

At the sound of the deadbolt turning, he turned back. Laurel opened the interior door, recognized him and unlocked the glass storm door, pushing it open. "Hi, Sheriff."

He knew a lot of attractive women, but something about this one had him taking notice and tamping down reactions he didn't care to acknowledge. "Joe."

She gave a brief nod of acknowledgement. "Joe."

The other night when he'd stood behind her to practice the alligator neck and escape move, the scent of her hair had pierced his chest with a jolt of awareness. Now again an ache formed around the vicinity of his heart. What was it about her that confused his senses and emotions? She seemed alone. She was obviously the wariest person he'd met outside of a jail, and something about the contrast of her extreme hesitancy and determined strength had won his interest— and his admiration. Her reticence piqued his curiosity. She'd been vague regarding anything in her past. "I won't take up your time. I came as a friend with an invitation. Chloe and I would like it if you came with us to my mother's for Thanksgiving dinner."

Her expression showed her wariness. The setting sun behind him highlighted her luminous pale skin and shiny dark hair pulled up in a messy knot of some sort. Even in an open flannel shirt with a plain blue tank underneath, she was incredible.

Her dark eyes showed her confusion, and he was prepared for her to decline the offer. She had no reason to fear him, but she didn't really know him. Her gaze dropped from his face to the insignia on his jacket, flitted only a fraction of a second on his hip—he was used to people looking for his weapon—but then her gaze lifted back to his face. She was thinking...wrestling with herself. He didn't want to stretch out the discomfort, and readied himself to tell her it was okay if she said no.

"Yes," she said finally. A one-syllable reply that seemed squeezed from her like the last bit of toothpaste from a tube. She shifted her weight fractionally, as though working to appear more confident with her answer than she felt.

"Great," he said, hiding his surprise. "It's casual. Nothing fancy. Chloe and I will come by and pick you up mid-morning that day."

"What can I bring?"

She wanted to bring something, so he didn't stall or tell her it wasn't necessary. "The Cavanaugh brothers and nephews love dessert. Anything sweet won't go to waste. Or even pre-meal snack food, like raw vegetables and dip."

"You snack before dinner?"

He gave her a sheepish grin. "All that cooking takes a long time. We watch football and play games while the meal is prepped. We're burning calories, and my mom doesn't let us eat the real food until dinner."

"How many others will be there?"

"I have twin sisters, two brothers who are married, one single brother, my grandmother and the kids. Not that many."

The lift of her eyebrows relayed she thought that was a lot of people, but she gave a little nod. "Okay."

"Do a lot of people make you claustrophobic? It's a big house, so we're not on top of each other."

"I don't think so," she replied.

Remembering what she'd revealed about herself the night they were locked in the *Herald* morgue, he asked, "It's the feeling that something bad is going to happen?"

She directed her gaze to his shoulder. "Something like that."

"You can have as much time as you need to acclimate and use your calming techniques. I'll help you any way I can."

"Thank you."

Another silence stretched between them. "Okay then, I'll be getting home. Have a good night."

"You too."

He turned and jogged down the stairs and got into his truck. She didn't know what she was getting into, obviously, and that made her uncomfortable. A nagging voice in the back of his mind asked what he was getting into himself. Chloe had instigated this, and Joe was more than willing to help his daughter develop a friendship. He didn't know whether or not to mention their neighbor's anxiety issues to his mom or let her figure it out. Liz Cavanaugh was a discerning woman, acutely sensitive to others. She would know how to make Laurel feel welcome in her home without his help.

He had a week to prepare himself.

❧

The sheriff's department was one of the historic stone buildings on Silverville Road, directly north across the street from Brook Park, the center of Spencer's town square. Across the side street to the east was Pearl's, the local hangout for the deputies and police, where steaming rich coffee flowed, and the latest gossip circulated. A few days after inviting his neighbor to family Thanksgiving, Joe was looking over budget sheets on his laptop, comparing them to the purchase orders on his desk. He could use a burger right about now, and conversation would distract him from this paperwork headache.

Office supplies and uniforms were always needed. The county required at least two new SUVs before the end of the year, half a dozen Kevlar vests and— He picked up a sheet of paper and unfolded it. Nearly every month somebody put in a request for a cappuccino machine. This one was signed by Jericho Tanner, a rock-solid officer and one of his best men. It was Vida who liked her fancy coffee, so he had his suspicions she was behind this organized campaign. Even though the coffee at Pearl's suited him just fine, he might have to buy them their damned cappuccino machine out of his own pocket.

All the phones in the building rang at the same time, an indication that a 9-11 call had come in. He reached for the receiver on his desk.

"Cavanaugh."

"Code three. 9-11 call from the high school." The voice was Chet Dalton's, the fire chief, which meant the call had come from east of here. Calls were routed to the nearest agency, and the fire station was closest to the high school. "Gunfire reported. Someone pulled the alarm. Teachers are evacuating."

"Copy in three." Joe jammed down the phone and grabbed the walkie on his belt. "Suspected shooting at Spencer High School. All available manpower code three. He grabbed his vest, rifle and Stetson and ran to the entryway, where Jericho Tanner and Mason Evans were already spilling from the common room with their vests. Tanner carried a shotgun. The others were out on patrol or answering calls and would join them. "Tanner, you take Lucas and Wick. Davies, Ireland and Evans, you're with me."

CHAPTER SIX

*J*oe was in full sheriff mode. His daughter was at the school, along with a couple hundred other kids, but his focus couldn't waver. He instructed Evans to call their off-duty officers for backup. North on Valleyview Road, the high school was on Timberline Trail, with the middle school across the street. To thwart any threat of the danger spreading, he called the middle school principal and ordered lockdown. "Officers will be there in minutes to watch the doors."

The fire department was about a minute ahead of them, their red and white SFD rigs already parked in front of the two-story brick building with two one-level wings out to each side and a glass atrium the full height front and center. Chet Dalton and two other officers stood in front of a rig. Dan Rivers and another paramedic were ready with the vehicle's rear doors open, backboards leaned against the bumper. Joe and Tanner pulled up close, the deputies jumping out.

"Students have evacuated west of the track," Chet told them. "Principal Hayes has all the teachers doing headcounts, and we'll have that report soon. I asked and your daughter is fine and accounted for."

"I appreciate that," Joe said, thankful to the man for having the forethought to immediately relieve that worry. "Where's Hornsby?" The police chief was notorious for not showing up for emergencies.

"MIA as usual," Officer Levi Ephram replied. "You lead. My teams will follow."

"Channel twelve!" he called loud enough to be heard by all the responders, then to Levi: "Send two men to guard the middle school while they're on lockdown." Joe assigned doors and lookouts. "Two-man teams sweep this building. Report your location every five minutes and state which rooms you've cleared. Put a lookout at each exit. We can't get in those doors, but someone could leave through them. I want that student headcount now."

Chet called Principal Hayes' phone and had a brief conversation. He shot Joe a nod. "All students are accounted for."

Joe let himself exhale a brief sigh of relief and nodded to the men. Levi assigned his officers, and the lawmen approached the school. With Frank Davies, one of his seasoned deputies at his side, Joe approached cautiously and entered the two-story sunlit atrium with the others. Two by two, the lawmen headed toward doors and hallways, while Joe and Davies proceeded forward to the locked office area.

He used his phone to call the principal. "These office doors are locked."

"The staff and I came out that way and locked them behind us."

Over the walkie on his hip, Ireland and Evans reported cleared rooms in the south wing on the first floor.

"The kids who were near the gym reported the shots were coming from there," the principal told him.

Joe hung up and motioned to Davies. They'd both been to countless games in that gym and knew the location. They cleared rooms along the way, reporting as they went.

His walkie crackled. "Found the source." The voice of an officer came over the air. "It wasn't gunfire. Firecrackers in the boy's shower area. Hell of a mess."

"Copy," Joe replied. "Teams, finish the sweep."

Half a dozen 'copies' responded.

Still toting rifles, he and Davies found the reporting team in the boy's shower area. Bits of what had obviously been firecrackers littered the room.

The patrol sergeant, Randall Voorhees, and another officer had discovered the scene. Voorhees gestured toward the restroom. "Check that out."

Joe approached the private green-tiled area with toilets and sinks. An entire divider had been blown off its moors, and a toilet lay broken on its side, completely ripped from the floor. Water spurted across bits of blackened porcelain.

"Holy shit," Davies said beside him.

"No wonder the kids were panicked," Joe said. "It had to have taken an M-80 to blow apart a toilet." He thumbed the button on his walkie. "Stand down. A toilet is blown to bits in the boy's locker room. Dalton, tell Principal Hayes to get a plumber out here asap to turn off the water. If he decides to send the students back in to finish the day, we're going to visit classrooms and see what we can dig up. Report back."

"Copy."

He and several of the officers exited the building from the west and headed toward the gathering of teachers and students milling on the synthetic surface of the oval competition track.

Phillip Hayes spotted them and walked forward to meet them. "Most of these kids are pretty shaken up," he said. "I don't know how much work they'd get done if they finished the day. I'm leaning toward early dismissal." He gestured with a thumb. "From the looks of Kit Carson Drive over there, ninety percent of their parents are already here anyway."

The long, curved drive named after a frontier legend, as well as Forest Lake Drive all the way south, were packed with lines of cars. Everyone had heard the emergency report, and worried parents had shown up. Joe and Levi exchanged a glance. Levi nodded.

"Sounds good," Joe agreed. "We'll have officers and deputies here tomorrow to talk to classes. If we get any leads, we'll go to students' homes. Every home if we have to. This wasn't funny." He looked at Hayes. "Anyone who might do this stand out in your mind?"

"We have a few troublemakers," he replied. "I'll make you a list."

"Dad!" Chloe came running across the expanse of brown grass, and Joe extended an arm to fold her against his side. She might be going on sixteen, but she still seemed small and frail to him. He hugged her, his hand engulfing her shoulder, and lowered his face to her hair. He held his whole world right here, and knowing she'd been afraid for even a short time tore at his insides.

He lifted his gaze to the over four-hundred other kids spilling across the track and school property. Some had spotted their parent's vehicles and left with them. "Do you have anything inside you want? I'm going to take you to Grandma's until my shift is over."

"My coat," she answered. "It's in my locker."

"Davies, will you take Chloe inside to get her coat while I talk to Principal Hayes? I'll meet you both at our vehicle."

"Sure thing, Sheriff. Come on, Chloe. Let's get your stuff."

His daughter released her hold on Joe and linked her arm through the crook of Frank Davies' elbow. She'd known the man since she was in elementary school.

"It makes me sick to think of how scared all these kids were," Joe said to Phillip Hayes.

"I'm right there with you, Sheriff," the principal said.

"When we find the student responsible, disciplinary action will be taken."

"I hope the discipline scares him as much as he scared all these kids," Joe said. "Because we're going to find him."

Levi had joined them. "Release the remaining students," he said, "and if any of them need rides, our men will see to it they get home."

Joe appreciated Levi's offer. "Deputies are on it." He turned to Phillip Hayes. "And then we're doing a locker search."

Principal Hayes nodded. "I'm on the same page. The counselors and security will help."

Hours later, Joe had never seen so many empty snack-size chip bags or half-empty soda bottles, and he could live the rest of his life a happy man if he never encountered another teenage boy's gym clothes. He and his search partner, the girl's guidance counselor, closed another locker. She inserted her key into the center of the combination lock and opened the next one.

Joe glanced back over the wall of lockers they'd just gone through and looked ahead at the remaining row in this hallway. The blue paint had been refreshed this year. There were four keys and about four hundred and fifty students, which meant each pair of law enforcement and school staff had well over a hundred lockers to search. And if nothing turned up here, there were more lockers in the boys' and girls' gym areas.

"Well, this is a nice change," his partner commented.

Joe turned his attention back to the task, immediately surprised by the clean, orderly contents of locker one-seventy-five. "Male or female?" he asked.

She took several papers stapled together from the pocket of her blazer and unfolded them. "Male. Koby Powell. A sophomore."

A neat stack of books sat on the top shelf, a stainless-steel water bottle beside it. Joe removed the lid and sniffed it. No smell. A hoodie hung on one of the hooks. The pockets were empty.

"Not even a gum wrapper." A first. "No sports clothing or gym clothes." He got on his haunches for the fiftieth time, and his knee shot pain clear through the joint and up his thigh. He grimaced, but kept the curse word on the tip of his tongue under his breath.

At the bottom of the metal cubicle was a notebook, and beneath it a metal box, like an old cashbox. Joe pulled it out and set it on the floor. It wasn't locked, and he lifted the lid. Inside was a bottle opener, a book of matches, two small butane lighters, a pack of cigarettes, two unopened red-wrapped packs of Black Cat firecrackers and a sandwich baggie holding six M-80s. "This is our guy."

"Stand back and let me snap a couple of photos, Sheriff." The counselor stood a couple feet back and used her phone to take pictures of the open locker and the lock box on the floor, as well as the contents.

Joe did the same. "Know much about this kid?" he asked.

"I'm the girl's counselor, but we have staff meetings to discuss issues, and Koby has been reprimanded for infractions of the code of conduct and contraband items more than once."

Joe called Principal Hayes, and a few minutes later he and Levi showed up.

After a brief discussion, the principal asked, "These items are definitely cause for disciplinary action, but the items themselves are circumstantial evidence, aren't they? This doesn't prove he caused the damage to the bathroom."

"It's rare that no one knows what a vandal is up to," Joe told him. "And even if no one saw anything, we can get him to talk." He said the latter with confidence. "I'll need his parents' names and information."

"Sure. I'll get it for you."

"Are we done?" Levi asked.

"I'd say we have what we need. What do you think?" Joe looked at the principal.

"That's enough evidence for me," Hayes responded. "Shall I call the Powells?"

Joe stood contemplatively, a hand at his hip. "I'd rather make a visit to their house now without the kid being prepared. That okay with you?"

"Yes, sir." Hayes tilted his head. "I'm more than happy to let you handle the parents. This is the least favorite part of my job. I'll go check on the plumbers."

Joe discussed an arrangement with Levi, and the law officials took their leave. He took out his phone on the way to his vehicle and texted his mom:

Leaving work late. Save me dinner?

She replied: Open-face hot beef sandwich waiting for you.

You're the best.

His youngest brother, Crosby was often there for dinner. Sometimes one or both of his sisters. He and Chloe were due for some family time, and it couldn't wait for Thanksgiving.

※

Another officer she'd never met filled in for Joe Cavanaugh at class that evening.

"Crazy day today," Piper Newport said from beside her.

"Was it?"

"Didn't you hear? The high school called in a shooter. It made the national news."

"No, I didn't have a radio or television on. What happened?"

"Thankfully, it was a false alarm. Some kid set off firecrackers and blew up a toilet."

"That's terrible."

Piper nodded her agreement. "Four hundred and fifty kids scared out of their minds, not to mention law enforcement wasting time and resources. Every cop, fireman, EMT and deputy in Spencer was on the scene."

"Do they know who did it?"

"I haven't heard."

The other instructor was a good teacher and led the training and exercises, but Laurel missed seeing Joe. Every day she had wrestled with herself about going to his family's for Thanksgiving. She had a lot to tell Dr. Easton. She'd gotten as far as exercise four and had changed her automatic reply from 'no' to 'yes', supposedly opening growth potential. Saying yes had taken every ounce of fortitude and determination she possessed, but the word had come from her mouth.

Even the sheriff had been surprised.

She had yet to follow through.

She didn't know his family. An entire entity of related people—mother, brothers, sisters, grandmother, nieces and nephews...her head didn't wrap around the picture. She'd had enough experience with individuals to know she didn't much like them as a rule. People were nosy, rude, condescending. What did that thinking make her?

Terrified.

She'd had a good reason for cutting herself off from prying eyes and questions. Self-preservation was all she'd known since she was ten years old. The protective cocoon she'd created was not easily breached.

At home later, she googled and saw photographs of all the county sheriff, police and fire vehicles in front of Spencer High School. How had Joe arrived and handled a call like that when his daughter had been a student in harm's way?

The same way he'd done everything else she'd seen him do, she supposed—calmly, matter-of-factly.

She made hot tea and watched television for a while before going to bed.

Laurel dreamed she was with Joe and Chloe Cavanaugh in an old-fashioned delivery van. They drove all over looking for firewood, but couldn't find anyone who had any to sell. As they got out of the vehicle in a wooded area, a huge, mangy dog approached them, its hackles up, teeth bared. The canine's fur was matted with blood. Laurel grabbed Chloe by the shoulders and guided her back to the truck, but Joe went forward, talking to the animal.

"Joe, let's go!" she called to him. "Get in the truck."

"The wood is all back there," he said and walked closer to the animal. He leaned down and reached forward.

Fear rose in Laurel's chest and she could barely breathe around it. Something terrible was going to happen. She couldn't sit here like a coward and let him be mauled. "Stay here. Don't move," she said to Chloe.

She got out of the vehicle and closed the door quietly behind her. The dog still growled menacingly. "Come back inside the car," she said to Joe.

"But the wood—."

"It doesn't matter now. Let's go."

"Are you afraid of everything?" Joe asked.

He was back in the vehicle, and was driving them toward a farmhouse. A canopy was set up on the lawn, and groups of people of all ages milled about, some playing games, others performing with instruments. Chloe found friends and left with them, but Joe led her to a woman at a potter's wheel, creating vases.

"Mom, this is Laurel," he said to the woman.

She had long gray hair and wore a shawl, and she squinted at Laurel. "So, you're the one?" she asked.

Laurel didn't feel welcome at all. It was clear everyone here knew about her. Others standing behind the gray-haired woman scowled.

"I'm Laurel," she said.

"You're not really Laurel," the woman answered. "We have a file on you." They were inside a canopy with canvas sides now, and the woman gestured to a row of old metal filing cabinets.

"How did you get those files?" Laurel asked.

"Jakob Spencer gave them to us. He knows everything about everybody."

Laurel turned to leave and Joe moved aside.

Standing in the opening, preventing her from leaving was the mangy brown dog, teeth bared, growling with menace. Panic overwhelmed her. She couldn't breathe. She tried to scream, but no sound came out.

Laurel jerked awake and sat up in bed, her heart pounding.

The dark room was silent. A sliver of moon shone through a crack in the curtains.

She calmed her breathing. What in the world? Was her discomfort over meeting Joe's family bringing on nightmares now? She'd spent years overcoming obstacles and changing her thinking and behavior. She'd come too far to let a few nerves get the best of her. She was Laurel Whitaker, contracted with Aspen Gold Lodge for the biggest project of her career. She wasn't intimidated by that fact. She had it under control and the money in the bank. She was taking classes and meeting people, working on self-improvement and confidence.

Admittedly Joe stirred up a lot of feelings, probably making her uncomfortable, but it was comfort that was her enemy, not discomfort. Knowing Joe led to improvement. She didn't know what safe felt like, but it was probably close to how she felt around him. Probably exactly how Chloe felt with him.

Feelings of expectancy and anticipation weren't easy to identify, but she lay back down and let herself feel them.

Expectation shouldn't be unwelcome, so she refused to let it manifest as fear. She wanted to see him again. She wanted to be free of everything that had held her back. She deserved freedom.

With everything in her, she wanted to meet his family.

&

Laurel cooked for herself, simple things that were easy to prepare. But she was nothing if not resourceful, so she googled ideas for Thanksgiving desserts and watched a few videos. Pretzel-chocolate-pecan slab pie stood out as not too complicated and sure to satisfy a sweet tooth. She shopped for all the ingredients, including bourbon and chocolate chips, but someone in the online marketplace had posted homemade cookies in pretty boxes for sale, so she picked up a couple orders of those just in case. The woman selling them lived in an 1800s home in a neighborhood west of Brook Park. If her own baked dessert was a fail, Laurel had a backup.

Thursday morning, her open-face pecan and chocolate chip dessert baked on a jelly roll pan turned out perfectly. After it cooled, she cut it into squares and placed them in a container. Her chest fluttered, but she took a deep breath. What was the worst that could happen? No one died of awkwardness.

Joe and Chloe picked her up as agreed, and Chloe sat in the back seat of the crew cab pickup so Laurel could sit in front. Father and daughter wore jeans, so she was comfortable with her choice of jeans, boots and an oversize cable knit sweater. The sun was unusually warm, so she hadn't worn a coat.

"Your boots are lit," Chloe told her immediately. "Did you order those?"

"I did. They're really comfortable."

"What did you make?"

"Pecan dessert bars. And I brought cookies."

"Wait until you try my Grandma's pumpkin pie. It's the best in the world, isn't it, Dad?"

He grinned at his daughter over his shoulder and caught Laurel's eye for a moment when he looked back to the road. "I haven't tried pies all over the world, but I'd wager it would rate right up there."

"I always help her whip the cream for the topping."

"I'm looking forward to watching that," Laurel said.

"Did you hear about what happened at my school?"

"I did, and I followed up online, but didn't catch any more news about it."

"This kid named Koby Powell blew up a toilet and set off a whole bunch of firecrackers in the boys' bathroom by the gym. We all thought there was a shooter. Everyone freaked. Girls were crying. We all went outside exactly like a drill and stood there while the firemen and police and deputies and my dad came. It's a lame plan, though, 'cause if there was a shooter, he could have shot us all standing there."

Laurel looked over and Joe met her glance. "She's not wrong. We're going over the evacuation plan so the students have more protection."

"That had to have been scary," Laurel said.

"It was *really* scary. I hope that tool Koby is expelled forever."

"What is the penalty?" Laurel asked.

Joe kept his eyes on the road. "He's being charged with aggravated assault, felony reckless endangerment and possession of a prohibited weapon. He's in the juvenile detention center in Denver, waiting on ruling and sentencing."

"Those are serious charges," Laurel said.

"And fitting the crime," he replied. "Someone could have

been seriously injured. It wasn't a practical joke. Students deserve to feel safe in their school environment."

"I agree." She turned in her seat to look at Chloe. "Are they offering counseling for the kids? Anything that affects your sense of security can lead to problems."

"We're talking about it in our SOAR groups. That helps, I think."

"What are SOAR groups?"

"The kids are all divided into small groups," Chloe explained. "Each group has eight kids from all grades together like an assorted family. We meet every other day as one of our classes, and we talk about stuff. You can do homework, too, if you want."

"A soar is a group of bald eagles," Joe told her. "Like a flock of birds or a pride of lions."

"Oh, so your school mascot is a bald eagle?"

"Yep," Chloe replied.

Vaguely she recalled her school having had a similar program, but she'd been excused from anything that made her uncomfortable. In hindsight that had probably been a mistake. "Very cool."

Joe turned into a long driveway that pulled around the back of an enormous house with dark green shutters and inviting porches. Behind the house was a multi-car garage and a gravel area for parking. Only two other vehicles were parked ahead of them.

"Kyle and Avery are here!" Chloe said excitedly.

"That's my brother, Tyler's vehicle. "The other is Crosby's," Joe added. "He usually picks up Grandma Naomi."

Laurel's stomach lurched. She sat taking long slow breaths before getting out of the truck.

"Are you all right?" Joe asked, coming around to snag the cookie boxes.

"I'm fine. I'm wearing my lit boots."

He grinned. "You made a joke. Tell me when or if you

need a time out," he said so only she could hear. "We'll take a walk or something."

His intuitiveness helped ease her discomfort. That, plus seeing him in a soft gray pullover shirt and jeans, made him fractionally less intimidating. "Thank you."

Chloe ran ahead and opened the back door. A chorus of greetings wafted to where Laurel stood outside on the deck.

Joe gestured for her to proceed him. She took a breath and stepped inside. He was right behind her. "This is Laurel Whitaker."

A slender woman with straight silver hair nearly to her shoulders hurried to greet her. "Welcome, Laurel. I'm Liz. Mom and grandma to this bunch. I'm delighted you've come to join us."

She took the container Laurel held.

"Thank you," Laurel said, meeting her friendly blue eyes. "I made pecan bars."

"And cookies," Joe said, setting the two boxes on the center island.

"Oh, I didn't make those," Laurel said quickly.

Liz pried up the lid of the plastic container. "Oh, my goodness."

A younger, slighter version of Joe approached and peeked at the dessert. "Oh, my goodness is right. Pretzels and chocolate chips? You're already a hit with this bunch."

"That's Crosby, my little brother," Joe said.

Crosby gave her a smile that made him look even more like Joe. He had the same eyes, the same full mouth and smile.

"This is my nephew, Kyle," Joe said, indicating a tall dark-haired teen. "And his sister, Avery." Avery wasn't as tall as Chloe, and Laurel guessed her a year or so younger. She wore jeans with threadbare knees and a loose-knit off-white sweater. Joe reached for a blond woman's hand and pulled her into a hug. "And this is my sister-in-law, Colette."

"Nice to meet you, Laurel." Colette pointed to a lower cupboard in a huge painted antique cabinet. "That's where we stick our purses."

"Okay. Thanks." Laurel stashed her bag with several others and closed the cabinet.

"Only a couple more to meet," Joe told her. "And then you can meet the others as they arrive." He indicated she should follow him along a wide hallway lined with family photos. They arrived in an enormous living area with multiple sofas and chairs. The wide-screen television was turned to a football game with closed captions, and the sound was off.

"Tyler and Gram, I have someone for you to meet. This is my neighbor, Laurel Whitaker."

Tyler's hair was lighter than Joe's, and he had a slenderer frame. He stood and reached to shake hands. He had a wide smile and his mom's bright blue eyes fringed with black lashes.

Their elderly grandmother sat on an upholstered chair. She wore a long floral skirt and red blouse with a long strand of pearls. "You're staying in a lake house?"

"Yes, ma'am. Mr. Rumford's property. I'm quite comfortable there."

"You can call me Naomi, sweetie. You're sure a pretty young thing. Isn't she Joe?"

Laurel's cheeks warmed more because the question was directed at Joe than because of the compliment.

"Yes, she is, Gram."

Crosby showed up with one of her dessert bars and seated himself. "I figured these were fair game, since Mom didn't have a chance to hide them. Delish, Laurel."

"I did warn you that my brothers are eating machines, right?" Joe asked.

She grinned. "You did."

"Do you want to sit here for a while or hang in the kitchen?"

"You relax and I'll go help with dinner," she answered.

"If you're sure."

"I'm sure." He didn't have to stay at her side. She might be uncomfortable, but he didn't have to spend his holiday babysitting her.

Back in the kitchen, she asked, "What can I do to help?"

"I don't want to give you the worst job," Liz said. "But these girls don't like peeling potatoes."

"I don't mind at all," Laurel offered.

"You're already my favorite," Liz told her.

"She says that to all of us," Chloe said.

Liz laughed and the others joined in. "Kyle, go into the pantry and get the bag of potatoes please. Laurel, you can use the sink at the island there, and there are paring knives and peelers in the drawer right beside the sink."

"I'll help," Colette offered.

Chloe and Avery stood at the other sink under the kitchen window, scraping carrots and cleaning celery, laughing about something one of them had said.

"Have you been in Spencer long?" Colette asked.

The pretty blonde wasn't prying. She was being friendly. People had a natural curiosity about each other. "A few months. Long enough to enjoy summer and fall on the lake. I've definitely seen what the tourists love about this place."

"Where did you grow up?" Liz asked.

Laurel fought down panic and counted to ten.

CHAPTER SEVEN

*I*t was natural for people to get to know each other by asking questions. These women were in no way a threat to her or her well-being. They were kind and friendly. "I lived in Arizona."

"I've visited," Liz said. "But the stark landscape can't compare to the lush beauty of the mountains."

"You're right about that," Laurel agreed. "But some would argue the climate is preferable."

"They would," Joe's mother said. "I'd go stir crazy without the transformation of seasons, though." She wiped her hands on a towel. "Have you seen the local sights?"

"I finally visited Olde Town, but I didn't make it very far."

"Is your family in Arizona?" Colette asked.

And now the family questions. "No. There's only me."

"Oh, I'm sorry, dear," Liz said quickly. "Well, I'm glad you're here with us today."

Apparently overhearing their conversation, Chloe spoke up. "Laurel has a really dope job. She's handles social media and makes websites for companies."

The others expressed their reactions. "I can barely keep up with my own social media," Liz said with a laugh. Without moving her lips, she said as an aside to Laurel, "In my day, dope was not a good thing."

Laurel hid a grin.

At the mention of her technical job, Kyle asked, "What are you working on right now?"

He'd perched on a stool and was munching a cookie.

"I recently signed a contract with Aspen Gold Lodge," she told him. "I'm designing an interactive website that showcases the lodge's features."

"Dope," he said.

Laurel and Liz exchanged an amused glance without comment.

Amidst the others' similar comments, Avery said, looking out the window, "Aunt Brooke is here."

A minute later, the back door opened, and a pretty young woman with black hair pulled back into a ponytail entered carrying a casserole dish. Chloe and Avery dried their hands and gave her hugs. "Aunt Brooke," Chloe said. "Come meet Laurel. She's our neighbor on the lake."

"Hey, Laurel," Brooke said, and then to everyone, "Yes, I made another green bean casserole."

"Perfect," Liz said. "Need to bake it before we eat?"

Another arrival showed up on her heels, this one a fair-haired little guy shooting in the door and hugging Liz around the waist. "This is Ian," Liz said and bent to kiss her grandson's forehead. The door opened again and Liz added, "And that's my son Dusty and his wife Kendra."

She recognized Dusty from her meeting at the lodge. "Hello again," he said with a smile.

She returned the greeting.

Kendra was stunning. She had gathered her mane of red hair at her neck and wore a coral blouse and slim jeans with a pair of white sneakers. She knew exactly where she fit in, and after the introductions, she donned an apron and headed for an adjoining room. "I'll start on the table."

Stephanie showed up next, a sleeker version of Brooke, with straight chin-length hair, camel-colored trousers and a cream silk blouse. She was even wearing heels and carried a large plastic tote containing two exquisite bouquets of flowers.

"Who died?" Dusty asked, and Steph pierced him with a mock glare.

"You know these are from the lodge," she said. "Fresh bouquets are delivered twice a week, and the old ones are tossed. Employees can take them home if we grab them in time. I salvage two or three at a time to make full new centerpieces."

Lodge goings on interested Laurel. "You work at the lodge too?"

"I do. I'm the event planner."

"Her talent spills over to us, too," Brooke said, returning from the dining room. "She's a control freak. Since she and I were about twelve, everyone's birthday parties have been over the top."

Laurel tried to imagine a twelve-year-old with the ability and means to plan family parties. Even trying hard, she couldn't remember a birthday party. She only knew her date of birth because after her mother's death, authorities had found her birth certificate in her mother's belongings. The date was the equivalent of a social security number to her—something that documented she was on the planet and accounted for.

"I'm not a control freak," Steph gave a shake of her head. "I'm organized. I simply prefer to plan and be prepared."

Brooke grabbed a carrot stick from the tray on the island. "That's what I said. Control freak."

Liz turned to Laurel as though gauging her reaction to the twins. The sisters were obviously very different, which seemed to amuse the rest of the family. Laurel had nothing to compare their relationships to.

Dusty had lighter hair than the other brothers and was every bit as handsome. They were all broad-shouldered and fit, and only Tyler and Dusty had their mom's blue eyes.

Joe joined them in the kitchen and hugged his sisters. He stood beside Laurel, picked up a chunk of raw potato and ate it. "You doin' okay?"

"I'm good." She glanced up to see the deeper question in his hazel-brown eyes. Her gaze unwittingly fell to his lips. She glanced away, meeting his mother's curious gaze.

"Hey, Uncle Joe." The fair-haired little boy, Ian came up beside them. "Is Laurel your girlfriend?"

To their credit, the Cavanaughs didn't miss a beat in their chatter or tasks, though Laurel was sure they'd overheard the child's question. Her cheeks warmed considerably, and she stared unblinkingly at the potato she was peeling.

In her peripheral vision, she was aware of Joe putting his hand on Ian's shoulder. "She's just my neighbor, buddy. And she's a stellar student in my self-defense class."

"Well, then maybe she can be Uncle Crosby's girlfriend. He didn't bring anyone."

Brooke and Stephanie lost their composure over that comment and Laurel looked up to see their shoulders shaking with laughter.

Dusty came over and curtailed the conversation. "Your Uncle Crosby doesn't need your help finding girlfriends, Ian. Neither does Uncle Joe. Let's go see if you can beat me at a game of checkers." The boy scampered ahead of him toward the other room.

"Crosby brings a different girl nearly every week," Joe explained. "That's why my sisters thought Ian's suggestion was hilarious."

"It *was* hilarious," Steph supplied. "Sorry, Laurel. Kids say whatever's on their minds."

Laurel hadn't been around children. She'd never been around a family either, so this whole day was surreal. What she *was* accustomed to was feeling awkward and out of place. She'd followed through with step four and had changed her automatic reply from a no to a yes. The worst hadn't happened. Yet. Supposedly, without any substantial proof yet, this was opening her up to growth potential. What was next?

Exercise five was sharing something about herself, rather than only listening and asking questions. She'd done that with Joe the night they'd been locked in the morgue at the *Herald*. She'd shared sensitive personal information about her fears and her therapy. She'd felt exposed and vulnerable, but had it helped? That remained to be decided.

She was good at therapy. She'd been in sessions since the age of ten, and she knew what therapists and counselors wanted to hear. This was different.

Before long she and Colette had ten pounds of potatoes peeled and cut. She rinsed them in the huge stainless-steel pot Liz had set out and then covered them with water.

"I think we can go relax until the turkey is nearly done," Liz announced, drying her hands and removing her apron. "Joe, will you open a couple bottles of wine for us, please?"

Joe opened the refrigerator, took out a red and a white wine, found a corkscrew and expertly opened them. Steph set out glasses and poured.

"Red or white?" Steph asked.

"I'll have a glass of white, thank you." Laurel accepted the stemmed glass and followed the others to the big room, where a football game was still on the television.

"Do you follow any teams?" Joe asked.

"Not really."

"The Dallas Cowboys have hosted a game every Thanksgiving for how long?" Joe asked, looking at Crosby.

"Forty-some years," his brother answered. "They usually wear throwback uniforms. They can't wear the authentic helmets though."

"Why not?" Colette asked.

"Now they have concussion protocol that wasn't in effect back then," Crosby answered.

"So what year are these costumes from?" Kendra asked.

All four brothers turned to stare at her.

"What?" she asked.

Dusty laughed. "They're *uniforms*, hon." He affectionately wrapped an arm around her shoulders. "Not costumes."

Kendra shrugged. "Same difference."

Laughter and friendly arguments broke out. Chloe and Avery took Kendra's side, and the brothers rolled their eyes. Crosby turned on closed captioning so he could read what the announcers were saying.

"We'll let Grandma Naomi decide," Tyler said. "Grandma, are the Cowboys wearing costumes or uniforms?"

The elderly woman waved her bejeweled hand and grinned. "What would your granddad say? Those are their Double Star jerseys. Those are *uniforms,* of course."

At the woman's response, Kendra laughed as hard as everyone else.

Brooke and Liz left the room occasionally, returning to join the conversations. Finally, Liz announced that dinner was ready.

"Grandma set a place for you between me and Dad," Chloe told Laurel.

In the dining room, the table was laden with steaming bowls of vegetables and mashed potatoes, and a long sideboard along the wall held casserole dishes, relish trays, pitchers of milk and bottles of wine. Tyler stood at one end and carved the turkey.

Joe pulled out a chair for her, and Laurel took a seat. He reached for her hand, catching her by surprise until she felt Chloe's touch on her right and realized everyone had linked hands. Tyler said a blessing over their food and thanked God for their health and family. She felt as though she'd been

transported into a Hallmark movie and couldn't resist
peeking at Joe beside her with his head lowered and eyes
closed. Would there be snow falling and a snowball fight
after dinner? The family members all said amens and immediately grabbed up bowls, served themselves and passed the
dish to the left.

Conversation picked up. "Arrest anyone lately?" Dusty
asked Joe.

"Nothing dramatic since the school incident. I did issue a
couple of warrants. Next week NIC is inspecting the jail, so
I'll be busy. No arrests though."

"Since that fiasco over the Michaels' ranch?" Tyler asked.

Laurel glanced at Joe beside her, and he obviously read
her curiosity. "Without going into details in front of impressionable dinner companions, I'll simply say for now that a
questionable filmmaker wanted a piece of land others were
buying and committed a couple of first-degree felonies in
trying to get it."

"The school thing was pretty scary though," Kyle said.

"You're right about that," Liz agreed.

"Since then I've read patrol logs for hours on end, investigated complaints, broke up a fight, did firearm training."

"And a lot of hammering," Chloe added.

"I'm doing inside framing now," her dad explained.

"I'll find a weekend before it's too cold and come give you
a hand with that," Dusty offered.

"Sure," Joe said with a nod.

Laurel had never seen so much food all in one meal,
except in ads and on television. She'd always wondered if
Thanksgiving dinner had been blown out of proportion, but
obviously not. The portions of food Joe and his brothers
heaped on their plates were astonishing, but explained the
amount of food that had been prepared. She glanced at Joe
from the corner of her eye. Did all men eat like that? Body
mass, physical activity, metabolism all obviously played a

part. But even teenaged Kyle stacked almost as much on his plate, including an entire turkey leg.

"Nobody makes potatoes and gravy like Grandma." Chloe savored a bite with her eyes closed.

"I second that," Colette said. "She had to teach me to cook when Tyler and I were married, but I'm still not as good as she is."

"Mom can't make steak fajitas like yours though," Tyler assured her.

Colette leaned toward him and he gave her a brief kiss.

Observing the obvious love these people shared as couples, siblings and family, an ache bloomed in Laurel's heart. Her memories of her mother were dim and overshadowed by trauma, but what she did remember were a string of boyfriends, alcohol-fueled fights and unending pans of orange macaroni and cheese. Foster care had been better, though the hierarchy of birth children and foster children fostered inferiority and bullying, and always moving to a new place right when the dynamic finally felt normal had taught her not to develop attachments.

Self-pity was not something she allowed herself. Life was what it was. Getting up each day and moving on was the only thing she could rely on. She was the only person she could depend on. Herself and a few dozen clinical therapists anyway.

"Did you grow up in Arizona, Laurel?" Liz asked, breaking through her thoughts.

Laurel set down her fork and folded her hands in her lap. The others grew unusually quiet.

She needed to share something about herself. It was what normal people did. It was what Dr. Easton expected her to do to improve. After composing herself and counting, she replied, "I went to college in Kansas and then in Illinois. More recently I lived in Arizona."

"So, you have a degree?" Stephanie asked.

"A couple of them," she answered. "Computer science and communications. Oh, and a bachelors in marketing."

"Working for the lodge should be a challenge."

Laurel nodded. "I'm really excited about handling Aspen Gold's online presence."

"I was there to hear her presentation," Dusty added. "Everyone was impressed with her ideas."

Laurel gave him a grateful smile.

"That's a really cool job," Avery said.

Laurel gave an embarrassed shrug. "I think so."

"Do you still have family in Arizona?" Liz asked. She was a kind, thoughtful woman, and she was curious, which was natural. She didn't intend to put Laurel on the spot.

This was the perfect lead-in to step number five. The question was her moment to respond with her own experience and share something about herself. Her heart fluttered, and she couldn't take more than a shallow breath. Beside her she felt Joe's intense presence.

She smoothed her napkin to occupy her hands. "My mother died when I was ten. There was no one else, so I was in foster care after that. I earned scholarships and worked my way through college. I actually paid off the last of my student loans with the signing check I received from the lodge. Signing that contract was the best day of my life."

She glanced over and met Liz's blue eyes which were disturbingly misted over. The woman gave her an encouraging smile.

"That might sound weird to all of you, but honestly, I'm good," she said directly to Liz. "I feel...accomplished."

"As you should," Liz assured her. "You have an impressive story for such a young woman."

Joe's mother had no idea about her story. None of them did.

"You are amazing," Stephanie said. "I'm still paying off my student loans, and I will be for a long time."

Joe's sister's casual praise caught her by surprise. She looked down at her plate. "I didn't do anything that plenty of other people haven't done."

"I disagree," Brooke said. "You did something even people with families to support them don't always do. And you did it on your own. I admire that. I admire you."

Laurel's nose and eyes stung with emotion. She swallowed hard and breathed evenly. She'd shared all that, and no ambulance had been necessary. "Well," she said with difficulty. "Thank you."

"No, thank you," Joe said from beside her. "For choosing to come to dinner with us. By setting an example for our impressionable kids."

She looked up and met his eyes. She read admiration and...something more in their hazel-flecked depths. Pride perhaps? Respect? She wasn't sure, but she liked what she saw, and her face and chest warmed.

Conversation and the meal proceeded around them. Joe smiled then, embarrassing her simply because she didn't know how to react. She smiled at strangers, but the action was fake and part of her built-in pretense to appear normal. But smiling at the person beside her who had shown her kindness and maybe admiration was so far outside her comfort zone, any reaction was in another zip code.

She gave him a nod and made an effort to savor the best meal she'd ever enjoyed. She'd never realized that the company of the right people could improve an already excellent meal.

Once everyone had finished, Joe and Tyler carried plates and flatware to the kitchen. She started to rise to help them, but Chloe put her hand on her arm. "The guys clear the table and make coffee."

"Wow."

"Wow is right," Colette said. "Mama Liz raised awesome sons."

They leisurely drank coffee, and anyone who wanted dessert was welcome to get up and serve themselves from the sliced pies and open containers. Crosby brought his grandmother a slice of pumpkin pie with a dollop of whipped cream.

"Gram and I made the whipped cream," Chloe told her great-grandmother.

Naomi tasted the dessert. "You did a good job. Come give me a hug."

Laurel was amazed that sharing something about herself had dispelled her anxiety. She'd spent her entire life being ashamed, hiding, avoiding. Her public childhood had been a nightmare of epic proportions. Nearly everyone who saw her or heard her name knew her story and looked at her as though she was a freak. She knew first-hand what pity looked like—and no one here had looked at her with pity.

Once dinner was cleared away and the dishes done, she played a couple of games of checkers with Ian. She didn't have to let him win, either—the kid was really good. When Chloe and Avery asked her and Colette to play a board game, she was embarrassed to admit she didn't know how to play. Liz joined in too, and Laurel admitted she'd never played Clue before. Avery didn't think anything of it and told her the rules. They let Laurel select her tiny plastic character first, so she chose the figure of Mrs. Peacock. Avery showed her how to keep track of the clues she learned on the scorepad and narrow down who committed the crime, and the game commenced.

Colette kept rolling elevens and twelves on the dice and ended up winning. Laurel won the second game, and then helped Liz serve dessert to those who hadn't indulged right after dinner—and also to the males who had. These Cavanaugh men were bottomless pits.

"I can't imagine how you fed four boys while they were

growing up," she said to Liz. "I didn't know anyone could eat so much."

"Teenagers are voracious." Liz tucked her shiny silver hair behind her ear with a laugh. "Now I only feed them like this on holidays, but Crosby moved back in here after my husband passed away, and he does outdoor work, so he still eats like that. The harder they play and work, the more they eat."

"It's a big house. I'm sure you're glad to have Crosby here."

She nodded. "He's here for most meals. Dusty and Ian used to come to supper all the time before he married Kendra. They actually lived with us for several years after he was born. Ian's mother gave Dusty custody as soon as he was born, so I took care of him while Dusty finished college and worked." She put on another pot of coffee. "I never know during the week when someone will text and say they're coming for supper, so I have to block out my own evenings when I want to meet friends. I just tell them ahead not to plan on me."

Laurel placed the lids on the dessert containers and wiped up crumbs. "I thought I'd feel far more out of place here than I do," she admitted. "I don't know anything about families—except what I've seen on television."

"I'm so glad you feel welcome. I have kind and generous children and grandchildren. We've figured out that families come in all shapes and sizes."

Chloe joined them. "Dad and Aunt Colette said Avery and I can spend the night if it's okay with you. No school tomorrow."

"Fine with me. You know the rules."

"We don't keep you awake laughing or playing loud music."

Liz grinned. "You've got it."

Just like that the girls were spending the night at their

grandmother's. Laurel had noticed before how at ease Chloe was with her dad, with inviting a stranger over, and today she'd seen her with her extended family. Now she knew how Joe and his daughter had become so welcoming and relaxed with a guest. It must be a comforting sense of security to be loved and accepted by an entire family.

"Each of the kids has their own toothbrush and pajamas here," Liz told her. "I have a lot of spontaneous visits."

"Sounds really nice."

By the time people started heading home, Laurel had learned to play Yahtzee with Joe, Kyle, Kendra and Dusty. "I'll take Grandma home in Mom's car," Crosby said. "It's easy for her to get in and out."

"I'll drive her home," Brooke offered. "My car is easy for her, and it's on my way."

The grandchildren all gave their grandmother a hug and Crosby helped her out to Brooke's car. Watching Joe's youngest brother attentively help his grandmother gather her things and then guide her out touched Laurel.

Joe hugged Chloe and his mom and, after Laurel had said goodbye, he escorted her out and opened the passenger door of his truck for her. He'd been pleasantly surprised when she'd openly revealed that her mother had died and she'd been in foster care. Previously she'd been so guarded and closed off, and he'd respected her privacy and hadn't asked questions. "My grandmother lives in assisted living now. It's a nice place."

"She seems like a great lady."

"She was never as warm or affectionate as my mom is with our kids, maybe because there were so many of us, or maybe it was her personality, but she had her own way. We visited her and my grandpa with my parents and she always had a little something for us kids. At Christmas she made us all flannel pajamas and bought us each a pair of slippers. Every year." He grinned. "She always kept Popsicles® in her freezer, and she let us play with the things in the trunks and boxes in their attic. It was great fun."

Laurel pictured the rowdy brothers playing in their grandparents' attic. She tucked away a blurry image of Joe as a kid. Maybe someday she'd see pictures. "It sounds nice."

He went around and got in on the driver's side.

"Your mom is great," she said. "Your whole family is really. I like them a lot. Thank you for inviting me. Or for going along with Chloe asking to invite me."

He was glad now that Chloe had initiated the invitation. "I'm glad you came."

At the first intersection, a neighbor coming from the other direction waved, and he raised a hand in greeting.

"I suppose you know everyone in Spencer."

"A lot of them."

"Being sheriff is an elected position, isn't it?"

"It is."

They rode in silence for several minutes. "That was the first time I've ever been to a family dinner."

Her admission was spoken softly, and he understood she was trusting him with something important. The sky was getting dark and the streetlights were on. "Not even with a foster family?"

He looked over as she watched the scenery roll past the side window. "It wasn't like that. I remember there were a couple of Thanksgivings with good food, but the foster kids ate in the kitchen while the family sat together in the dining room."

Joe got an ache in his chest at the thought of a child feeling unwelcome or unwanted in any way. Images of lonely children in his head now, he cursed under his breath. Refusing to feel pity for this determined young woman, he cleared his throat. "I don't know how people can treat kids like that."

"It's easy for them. They let the child live under their roof, and they cash the check."

His childhood had been a ride on easy street, and he'd known it, but the facts screamed at him now. "But surely there are good foster parents out there who actually want to help kids."

"I hear there are. I know there are social workers who want to help and who do their best, because I've met them. But the system is overcrowded and underfunded and even though they follow up, they can't be assured who is or isn't a good caregiver with an unselfish motive. It is what it is."

"You sound more resigned than resentful though."

"I guess I am."

"Anything you want to ask about me or my family?"

She glanced over at him. "Not really."

"Not curious about anything?"

"Maybe, but I don't ask personal questions."

He wanted to keep the give and take of information flowing between them. "It's okay. Ask me something."

"Well. You mentioned that your brother Dusty and his wife Kendra have only been married a few months. Your mom said something about Dusty getting custody as soon as Ian was born."

"Right. Ian isn't Kendra's biological child." He turned onto Highway 34 toward their side of the lake. "This is going to sound a little out there, but you'll hear it somewhere, so better to hear it from me than as gossip. Ian is Kendra's sister's child." He let Laurel analyze that for a minute. "After high school Dusty and Kendra were engaged, and Erica Price put something in Dusty's drink in order to have sex with him. We only learned the truth recently. She'd done the same thing to other guys. Dusty couldn't remember anything, but the DNA testing proved Ian was his. Erica didn't want a baby. She signed over her rights immediately."

"Wow. You hear about men doing that to women, but I've never heard of a woman taking advantage of a guy like that."

"It happens."

"Did she get caught?"

"She was discovered, but she died before a hearing could take place."

"That's terrible." She glanced over at him. "Dusty and Kendra sure seem happy together now."

"They were always meant to be together. Fortunately, she owned the house on the other side of you, and she came back to Twin Owl Lake every summer. One thing led to another, they realized they still loved each other, and then they learned the truth."

"I'm happy for them."

"Me too." He pointed to the side of the road. "A fox."

The small animal's eyes glowed in the headlights before it ran into the trees. Joe turned on the radio. She recognized a song she'd heard several times.

Today had been eye-opening. Laurel was glad she'd accepted their invitation and gone to the Cavanaughs. The closer they got to the lake house, the more the words of the song bore into her thoughts. *'No one's there, no one's around, just this land and just this house. No sound, no fuss, no people waiting up. It's just us, dear nighttime.'*

The chorus coming up glorified freedom. At one time she'd identified with those words and probably used them to justify being alone and accountable to no one. She wasn't so sure anymore. Freedom didn't necessarily mean being alone. Alone was simply alone—lonely for the most part, no matter how she dealt with it or covered it up or assured herself it didn't matter. It did.

'No people waiting up.'

"I don't have much to offer." When he looked over, she quickly explained. "I mean, I have coffee or tea. Would you... would you want to come in for a cup of coffee?"

CHAPTER EIGHT

*H*er heart was in her throat. The invitation was completely out of character and out of her comfort zone. If he said no, she'd probably melt in a puddle of relief.

"That would be great. Sure," he replied.

Well, she'd done it now. She nodded and unfisted her hands. "Okay."

He parked in the drive, and she got out on her own. He followed her to the door. After fumbling with her keys, she got the door open, set her bag and container on a table and reached for the switch to turn on the lamps.

"This looks a lot different than I remember," he said. "When Ben lived here, the place was pretty rustic. It's all new."

"I like it."

He followed her into the kitchen, where she pulled a basket of coffee pods forward.

"Flavored or plain?"

"Plain for me, thanks. I'm not a fru-fru coffee person."

She filled the container on the coffee maker with fresh water. "Is fru-fru a word?"

He grinned. "My sisters use it."

"I like them both. I didn't realize one of your sisters was a lodge employee."

"Yep, she's on staff. And Brooke is a trauma nurse, trained for flight rescue."

"Amazing. They're both beautiful and smart, but so different from each other."

He chuckled. "Couldn't be more different."

"Four sons and then twin girls. What a wonderful addition to your family. Quite an adjustment for your parents after all the boys."

"They came to us on purpose, actually. My folks adopted them when they were infants."

"Oh, I had no idea. That's even better."

"They were left at the fire station, which back then wasn't even a thing like it is now. The abandonment made the local news, and the fire chief at the time was my mom's cousin. After the babies were checked out at the hospital, he made arrangements for her to take care of them until the authorities figured out what was going to happen. My whole family fell in love with those two dark-haired little girls, and that was that."

"Anything in your coffee?"

"No, black, thanks."

She handed him a full cup. "It probably took quite a bit of legal work wading through red tape, searching for a relative, going through child protection services, and all that."

He glanced at her. "I was young, so I don't remember all the details, but I do remember the day we all went to court for the adoption. My mom has the clipping from the feature in the *Spencer Herald* the next day with a photo of our whole family and the judge."

Laurel smiled. "That's pretty incredible. I'd like to see that photo."

She sipped her own coffee and considered asking him to sit. In here? Out in the other room?

"When you were playing games with the kids, that was the first time I'd seen you really smile." He took a sip of his coffee. "You have a great smile."

She didn't know what to say. She lowered her head and looked at her cup. "Thanks." After pursing her lips and taking a breath, she glanced up. "Want to sit in the other room and be comfortable?"

"Sure."

She turned and led the way to the living room.

He stood on the stones in front of the hearth. "You don't use the fireplace? It's clean and there's no wood."

"There's wood outside. I have no idea how to make a fire, and fire making is likely too dangerous for a novice."

"You didn't google it?" He looked at her with that amused expression he and his siblings got when they teased each other. He'd mentioned more than once that she didn't think he was funny.

She got his jest this time. "Actually, I did, but there were conflicting instructions."

He set down his coffee mug. "How many ways can there be to start a fire?"

She shrugged. "Several, apparently."

"Do you want to learn? I'll show you."

"Sure."

"Okay." He rubbed his palms together. "Do you remember seeing anything that looks like a firewood sling? Probably canvas with handles or straps."

"Oh, I do. It's in this coat closet." She got the sling and unfolded it.

"I'll be right back. Can you find some newspaper or paper? Shredded would be perfect. And a lighter or matches."

She didn't buy newspapers, but she had a small paper

shredder on a wastebasket in the other room, so she grabbed a big handful of scraps.

He returned with a few short pieces of split wood with the bark still on and a small pile of twigs. "So, first thing you do—and never forget this step or you'll be sorry—is open the flue." He twisted the brass key on the front of the brick fireplace and a metallic squeak sounded from inside the fireplace. "That's what keeps out weather and animals, so it's shut when not in use, but if you forget to open it, all the smoke will back up into the house."

"Got it."

He hunkered down in front of the opening. "Okay, come watch."

She knelt beside him at a comfortable distance, but his woodsy cedar scent reached her, awakening memories of their confinement that night at the *Herald*. Her senses went on alert.

"Our key components to getting fire are wood and air. So first we use these small pieces that will catch quickly. You sort of stack them up like a tipi on the grate. He broke pieces over his knee and arranged them. "Keeping lots of air in between them." Once he had a little tower built, he picked up the bigger pieces of wood.

She watched his hands as he worked, fascinated by their size and the way his wrists flexed. It was impossible not to notice the thickness of his arms and the movement of muscle under his knit pullover. The vivid memory of lying behind him that long night in the *Herald* morgue played through her head. He'd been assured, strong, warm. She'd felt safe.

"We want to put these bigger logs in front-to-back, so if they roll, they won't roll forward out of the fireplace. Now I can add another one the other direction to the top, because it has a good base, but they're not close together and there's a lot of air between them."

He glanced at her.

Had he caught her looking at him? "Okay."

"This shredded paper is perfect. If you didn't have this, you could peel paper into strips. You don't want a big wad because it won't catch as easily." He grabbed a handful and shoved it underneath the grate below all the wood he'd arranged. "Now all we do is light it."

She handed him a packet of matches.

"Pick up a grill lighter. They're safest because you don't have to get as close." He struck a match and held it to the paper strips until several caught fire. Shaking out the match, he tossed it onto the pile.

The shredded paper burned quickly, the heat reaching them, and then the sticks caught fire, snapping and cracking pleasantly.

She watched, admiring how easy he made everything look. "The paper starts the sticks burning, and the sticks start the logs burning."

"Exactly. Once the fire's going well, you want to keep the screen in front of it, so sparks don't fly out into the room." He set the black screen in place.

At least she had an excuse for the warmth in her cheeks now. "That's nice. Thanks for showing me."

"You're a quick learner."

Now, with him looking at her and both of them kneeling before the fire, their nearness seemed awkwardly intimate. But what did she know? She felt awkward about everything, and yet this was the best awkwardness she'd ever experienced. He wasn't looming over her or threatening in any way. He was one of the kindest, gentlest people she'd ever met, though she knew he was tough and aggressive at his job. That juxtaposition of strength and peace struck a chord and peeled away a papery layer of her fear and distrust.

She looked into his eyes. What did he think of her? The blaze now gave off enough light to highlight his features, the deep bow of his upper lip…the disquieting fullness of the lower one. He terrified her—or her reaction to him terrified her; in either case, her legs trembled, and she shifted her weight to rest with a hip solidly beneath her.

"What are you thinking?" she asked.

"Do you really want to know?"

"Yes.

"I was thinking you're the most beautiful woman I've ever known. Strong, but feminine. Smart." His gaze took in her hair, her eyes, her mouth. "And now your question made me realize that you don't play games."

"Games?"

"You don't flirt. You look directly at a person. You hold a lot inside, but what you do say is out there. No games."

"Not the sort of woman you're used to, I guess."

"You're like no one I've ever known, that's for sure. And that's a good thing."

She raised her eyebrows. "It is?"

"It is. What were *you* thinking?"

She rubbed her thumbnail against her jeans. "I was…I was wondering what you were thinking about me. And now I know. Possibly."

"What were you thinking about me?" he asked.

His steady gaze called her out, so she turned and looked at the fire. "I was remembering the night we were locked in at the *Herald.*"

He didn't press her for more, but adjusted his weight to a sitting position.

"You really think I'm beautiful?"

"I thought it from the first time I saw you."

"Joe."

"Yeah."

A question was burning in her, the issue hotter than the fire. Her heart pounded, and she couldn't believe she was going to say the words, but she couldn't not. "Am I someone you would kiss?"

She made herself look at him to gauge his reaction.

His eyes seemed to darken even more, and the firelight reflected in their depths. "Seems like you're fast becoming the only someone I want to kiss."

He leaned toward her and she met him, their lips touching softly like a tender test, and then he tilted his head and covered her lips more fully. Everything about this moment felt right—the warmth of the fire, the sweet expectation, the delightful sensation of his lips on hers. She moved only enough to study the planes and angles of his cheeks and jaw, the arch of his brow, the shadowed divot above his lip.

He reached up to test a strand of her hair between his thumb and fingers, push it behind her ear, rest his palm along her jaw. "Don't stop."

She pressed her lips to his, instinctively threading the fingers of one hand into the thick silken hair at the back of his head. She experienced every life-changing second, every beat of her heart...every nuance of his warm lips. She couldn't breathe, couldn't think, couldn't wrap her head around kissing Sheriff Joe Cavanaugh, but her senses took over and knew what to do.

Kissing him felt right. Good in ways she hadn't anticipated. The first time she'd seen his silhouette, his size and muscled form had stolen her breath in a terrifying manner. She wasn't afraid of him in this moment. He'd shown her only kindness, demonstrated care and tenderness with his daughter, toward his family. He taught women how to protect themselves from men who meant them harm.

His firm lips were an indulgence she gifted herself, a gentle caress she'd yearned to discover. The only thing that terrified her now was herself. Her naïveté, her awkwardness, the reactions she couldn't control...he likely viewed her as an interesting oddity—a puzzle to figure out. He'd be sorely disappointed once he realized there were pieces missing. She was incomplete.

She let her fingers slide from his hair, graze his shoulder briefly, and she moved back to look at him.

She adored looking at him.

The only sound for several minutes was the crackling fire. Finally, he said, "I have to get up before I can't."

He stood, putting his weight on his left leg, and stretched out his right, bent it at the knee a couple of times. She'd noticed his faint limp the morning after they'd slept on the floor of the paper morgue. He reached for her hand and helped her up.

"Did you injure your leg?" she asked.

"Years ago," he said. "Took a bullet."

He'd talked about doing paperwork and reading shift reports, but his job could turn dangerous at any moment, and surely it had many times over the years. His mother must have learned to live with that knowledge, as had his daughter. Caring for someone, loving them, meant concern, sometimes fear.

She felt small with her hand in his much larger one. But she also felt safe. It was a unique sensation, something she surely shouldn't get used to. She took care of herself, always had. But she wanted nothing more than to rest her other hand on his broad chest, step close against him and know how it felt to have him wrap her in his arms. She felt light-headed at the thought. If she reached out to steady herself, he would enfold her. She had no doubt. She could rest her head against his large firm body and absorb his warmth and peace.

She closed her eyes. Withdrew her hand.

Joe reached for his mug on the table, perched on the edge of the sofa and finished his coffee. If he wasn't careful, this woman could get under his skin in a big way. Everything about her was different from anyone he'd ever known—and the feelings she stirred in him were different, as well. He had no business getting himself coiled up inside over a woman he barely knew.

She didn't share much of her past and held her personal life in reserve. That was fine. The more he knew, the more he'd have to deal with. Her silence about her past could mean a lot of things. An abusive boyfriend or husband was his first guess. Excessive privacy and anxiety were often signs of domestic abuse. Her low profile could indicate she was hiding from someone. When he'd shown up in uniform the night of the storm, it had been apparent she'd struggled to remain calm and not show fear.

And she was taking a self-defense class.

If she was in trouble and needed help, he couldn't ignore it.

His gut instincts told him he'd put his foot straight into a steaming pile of trouble.

And he wanted to kiss her again.

❦

The next morning Joe sat down at his desk with a cup of coffee. Sometime or another his fellow officers had amused themselves by replacing his mugs. This least obnoxious one read '10-4 COFFEE THAT.' He sipped and read through his email.

Having thought it over for a week or so, he pulled up a shopping site, read recommendations, and ordered a damned cappuccino machine on his own credit card. Maybe he'd earn enough flight points to take Chloe somewhere. Spencer was a smorgasbord of fun activities, but when a kid lived here, they still needed to see a bit more of the world.

After ten minutes of non-productivity, he realized he'd still been thinking about Laurel Whitaker. He typed her name into several databases available to him. She had no criminal activity associated with her name. Her first driver's license had been issued in Florida when she was twenty-four. Seemed odd, but some young people didn't drive immediately. He located no college records until she was a junior. She'd achieved a bachelor's degree in marketing at Indiana University in Bloomington. She'd also gone to University of Virginia in Charlottesville. With the two degrees she'd mentioned, that probably made sense, but why two entirely different colleges in two states? And neither had anything to do with Arizona. Or Florida. She'd said she had no family, but everyone came from somewhere.

He was uncomfortable researching her. She obviously valued her privacy. But if something was wrong—if she was afraid of someone, he should know. By not knowing a crime or a threat, he was going about this search backward, but that wouldn't matter. He had contacts. County sheriffs across the nation participated in a network for communication.

First, he delved into the Victim Assistance Network, searching for anything he could find connecting her as a victim, also using her description and then flagging the few known states. By lunch he had nothing.

He sent an email to the County Sheriffs Network, requesting that participating counties search for records of a victim with her name or description in a domestic abuse report. It could take days for responses. He grabbed his coat and hat.

A minute later, he stepped out of the cold into the warmth and permeating coffee smell at Pearl's Café and was immediately greeted by several neighbors. Loydelle Hendershot, the postmaster was sitting with redheaded Emily Davis, the office manager who worked across the park at the veterinary clinic.

"Coming to the fish fry Friday night?" Loydelle asked. "I haven't seen you there for a while."

"That sounds good," he replied. "Chloe and I will have to make it a date."

He hung his coat and hat in the back office, where Uncle Bud saved space so the lawmen's things were out of sight, then sat at the counter with the fire chief, Chet Dalton and police officer, Levi Ephram.

"Still no news about that Powell kid," Levi said. "When was his sentencing supposed to be?"

"Sometime this week I was thinking," Joe answered.

"Hey, Joe. What will you have?" With her usual cheerful smile, Piper Newport set a glass of water and a roll of silverware in front of him. She took her order pad from her apron pocket. "Hot beef sandwiches are the special today. Or Bud can grill you up your favorite burger."

"The hot beef sounds good," he said.

"Coffee?" she asked.

"I'll have a couple glasses of milk, please."

"Sure thing." She tore the order from the pad and clipped it on the carousel above the serving window open to the kitchen and returned with his milk. "Looking forward to class tonight. It's kind of fun."

"Well, you're an excellent student."

Smiling, she turned away with a swing of her blond ponytail.

He glanced over to see Levi grinning at him. "Great way to be a chick magnet, right? Teach them to defend themselves and show them how sensitive you are."

"Hey, I'm a sensitive guy."

"You know, I believe that." With a grin, Chet tossed several bills on the counter beside his plate and stood. "In fact, I've personally seen you hug a guy after giving him a citation."

"Don't you have an inspection to make?" Joe asked.

They laughed and Chet went for his coat and exited the café. Levi followed him out.

Joe was finishing the last of his potatoes and gravy when a strong arm wrapped around his shoulder and then released him. Crosby dropped onto the stool beside him and set down his laptop on the counter. "Hey, big brother. Had some down time, so I came in to grab a booth and work on my website. Saw you over here."

"You do your website yourself?"

"Sort of. I had it designed, but I limp through adding photos and doing updates. The whole thing needs an overhaul."

"Laurel could help you out. That's what she does. You should give her a call."

"I thought maybe the two of you had something going," Crosby said.

"Geez, Crosby, I wasn't suggesting a hook-up. She could help you with your business and marketing."

"So, you *do* have something going with her?"

"No. Maybe." He tossed down his napkin.

Crosby raised his eyebrows, probably to irritate him.

"Hey, Crosby." Piper had shown up with her order pad.

"Hi, Piper." He jerked a thumb at his brother. "I'll have what he had."

"Two glasses of milk?"

Crosby glanced at Joe's empty glasses. "Sure."

Piper glanced over their heads at someone entering the café. She pointed to the stool beside Crosby.

Brianna Jamison hung her coat on an empty booth hook and came over to greet them. She wore slim jeans and a red-and-white striped cable-knit sweater with a wide neck that exposed one shoulder. "Hey, Cavanaughs," she said with a smile and studied Crosby. "Hi, Cros."

"I'm leaving," Joe told her. "You can have my seat."

She and Crosby had dated off and on for a few years, and she'd been to several of their Sunday dinners. She was fun to be around and had always seemed pleasant. Crosby never dated anyone for long, so the fact that they often came back around to each other must be seeded in friendship.

"Oh, I'm meeting someone," she said. "But thanks. How's your newest sister-in-law doing? She seemed to fit right in."

"Kendra's great," Crosby answered.

Joe took money from his wallet and pushed it across the counter with his ticket. "Good to see ya, Brianna. Later, Crosby."

On his way back from retrieving his coat, Brianna was sliding into a booth across from a vaguely familiar twenty-something guy in jeans and a Broncos hoodie over a t-shirt. A glance at Crosby clued him in that his brother's casual on-again off-again relationship with the raven-haired girl might not be so casual on his side. He'd wondered.

He pulled on his hat and zipped his coat shut. He wanted to get back and see if he had any email replies yet.

CHAPTER NINE

*L*aurel had signed up for a couple of mailing lists and got news of the First Friday Celebration at Old Stone Church. It was a Christmas theme, with a pricey admission fee to enjoy wine and hors d'oeuvres, as well as support the co-op. Her first inclination was to delete the email, but changed her automatic reply to yes and purchased her ticket online. She owed herself a true celebration for her Aspen Gold Lodge contract and for achieving several of her challenging steps.

She read the entire invitation and even looked up the social media announcements and found photos of their other events on the website. All appeared pretty fancy. Without time to order something online, she bundled up in a long coat and boots and visited the boutiques along Brook Park Road.

She bought more than one ensemble and put off deciding which to wear until the last minute. She chose an emerald green tea-length skirt, with a black sleeveless lace shell and a matching green patent belt. Black heels completed her outfit. She hot-rolled her hair, which was quick and easy and created long waves, then left it down over her shoulders. For jewelry she chose only silver hoop earrings and a silver bangle bracelet. She felt as confident as was possible as she put on her coat and left the house.

After pulling onto Old Church Street and spotting the stone church building, an attendant at the entrance showed her where to park. The lot was already a third full, and blue lights outlined the entire historic building. She stood outside on the pavement a moment. What was the worst that could happen?

Another attendant opened the door, and the mellow voice of Bing Crosby singing *I'll Be Home for Christmas* welcomed her. The gentleman took her e-ticket and explained where to check her coat. A few minutes later, she came back into the entryway and got her bearings.

Tall silver vases filled with birch logs and evergreen branches stood on either side of the double doorway into the main room. The center area was a forest of plain and flocked Christmas trees, each one lit and decorated differently and bearing a tag identifying the decorator. The entire building smelled like mulled cider and spruce, a pleasant sensory experience.

"Hello," a slim silver-haired woman in a shapely blue dress and floral neck scarf greeted her. "Welcome to the Artists' Cooperative Gallery. Have you visited before?"

"Yes, I have. I'm on the mailing list."

"Delightful. I'm Willa Samuels-Spencer."

"I remember your paintings from my visit," Laurel replied. "They're all lovely." This was the woman who had resourced funds to make this co-op happen. "It's a pleasure to meet you. I'm Laurel Whitaker. I rent on the east side of Twin Owl Lake." She filled in that information since everyone always asked.

"Yes, of course. You're my husband's most recent discovered treasure."

"Jakob Spencer is your husband?"

"As of one week," she replied with a pleased smile.

"I don't know about the treasure part, but I can tell you it's the best job I've ever had the privilege of taking on."

"I'm delighted for you," Willa said. "And for the lodge. The stuffy old place needs new blood and fresh ideas to keep it relevant. You, my dear are just the ticket."

"Well, I hope so."

"Come, let's get you a drink, and I'll introduce you to my friends."

Laurel found herself taken under Willa's wing with a glass of wine in her hand. She met a few of the co-op's benefactor's and members of the Spencer Historical Society, including Aunt Cora. The friendly woman said she'd love to meet and answer questions about Spencer.

Tall dark-haired Ryder Barlow had familiar green eyes. "Ryder is my new grandson, now that I've married his grandfather," Willa told Laurel. That explained the green eyes. "And this is his lovely fiancé, Vianna."

The curvy young woman beside him smiled. She wore a bright smile and had short black hair that curled charmingly. "Hello, Laurel. I love your skirt. You look stunning."

The compliment took her aback. She formed a proper response, going for normal conversation. "Thank you. I got everything I'm wearing at the boutiques near the park downtown."

"Well, you are Christmas elegance," she said.

Laurel returned her smile and sipped her wine.

Jakob Spencer joined them, slipping his arm around Willa's waist. The older woman smiled up at him, and Laurel sensed the loving connection between them.

"You look lovely this evening, Laurel. I'm delighted to see you here supporting my wife's cause."

"Thank you, Mr. Spencer. Spencer is making a big difference in my life. I'm honored to participate in this small way."

"Not so small," Willa told her. "The co-op gives artists of

all levels of experience an opportunity to show the community their gifts. Spencer has a million tourists each year, and a good many of those visit Olde Town. Now they will be exposed to the artists we celebrate here."

"That's amazing," Laurel said.

"I see you're meeting some of my family," Jakob said. "If my daughters aren't here, they should be arriving soon. Excuse me, I want to greet one of the benefactors."

"Enjoy the food and drinks," Willa said and followed her husband.

"Still can't believe they're newlyweds," Vianna commented.

"After all these years, it's about time," Ryder said. "Do either of you recognize that young woman?" he asked. "I usually know everyone at these events."

The attractive woman he mentioned was of average height, her wavy mahogany-colored hair pulled back with rhinestone-studded combs. She wore a plum-colored wraparound sheath dress with matching shoes. At the same moment they observed her, she glanced away from the person she was speaking to and spotted their attention. Her hesitant smile prompted Ryder into action. He left Vianna's side and strode over to her. A moment later, he led the newcomer to where Vianna and Laurel stood.

"This is Matt Chandler's sister, Whitney Chandler." He made the introductions, and then explained to Laurel, "Matt owns and runs Timberline Outfitters. He has a stable full of horses and does trail rides. Whitney grew up here, too."

"It was past time I come visit my nephews," she said. "I wanted to get here during the summer, but I had an especially busy season. I hadn't seen them for almost a year, and that's far too long."

Vianna leaned back to glance between her fiancé and the newcomer. She pointed with her forefinger while holding her wine glass. "So, you are both related to Zach and Stevie."

Ryder explained, "Nikki was my cousin, so they're my first cousins, once removed."

"How did you figure that out?" Whitney asked.

"Sometimes at a gathering, we cousins bend our minds around how everyone is related," he answered. "During the summer, Matt sometimes brings the boys to Friday nights in the park."

"That's good. They need to know family." Whitney had a wholesome look about her, wore very little make up, but her large hazel eyes didn't need help. Laurel assumed from the conversation that Ryder's cousin had passed away.

"I love what the co-op is doing with this place," Whitney said. "They've preserved the history of the building and are using it in a fresh new way while featuring local artists. Are either of you artists?"

"I make hand-made paper, create journals and paint covers," Vianna replied. "I also hand-make greeting cards. I had a display here this past fall."

They glanced at Laurel.

"Oh, no, I'm not artistic. My designs are all virtual. I design websites and help companies with social media marketing."

"And just landed a contract with the lodge," Ryder added.

"Yes, that," Laurel said with a shy shrug.

"Congratulations." Whitney raised her half-full glass. "Here's to wowing their winter socks off."

The three touched glasses and took sips.

"You know, I'd love to get your card and talk to my board about web promotion," Whitney said to Laurel. "My organization isn't on a scale comparable to the lodge's, but I hope you'd consider us anyway."

"Yes, of course." Laurel dug in her clutch for a business card. "What is it you do?"

"I'm a curator for The Hadley Textile Museum in Boise."

"Quilt collections?" Vianna asked.

"Actually, we were among the first museums to exhibit quilts as works of art. Our collections feature masterpieces from New England, the Mid-Atlantic, the Midwest, and the South and include Amish, appliqué, chintz, crazy, pieced and whitework. But over the years we've expanded to needle-work, rugs, printed fabrics, hats and more. It's an amazing assortment of crafts."

"It sounds fascinating," Laurel said. "I'd love to see it. And I'd love to do work for your museum. That would give me a good reason to travel to Idaho." She handed Whitney her card.

"You'll hear from me," Whitney said. "Excuse me. I want to greet Willa."

After she'd stepped away, Vianna told Laurel, "Ryder's cousin Nikki killed herself a few years ago. It was tragic."

"Oh, I'm so sorry," Laurel said.

"Her husband, Matt, took it hard," Ryder said. "She'd always had her ups and downs, but no one expected that."

"Let's go check out the food," Vianna suggested.

Laurel nibbled a few hors d'oeuvres and met Ryder's lovely mother Zoe, who ran a bed and breakfast. Standing back to observe the crowd, she experienced an odd sensation, as though she was watching herself meet people and talk to them, so out of character and usually stress-inducing. She'd had a few qualms and had forced herself to converse, but she hadn't felt the customary anxiety.

What was the worst that could happen? She might say something stupid or spill cocktail sauce on herself.

A guest across the table dropped a cube of cheese on the floor and nudged it under the table with the toe of her sparkling silver pump. Laurel grinned to herself and turned away so the woman wouldn't glance over and see she'd been observed.

In one way she felt embarrassed for the woman, but in a different way, she felt exonerated. The woman had been pretty casual about the mishap, and rightly so. People dropped things all the time. The possibility of something unexpected wasn't paralyzing to normal people.

In the background, Eartha Kitt sang *Santa Baby* while guests nibbled cucumbers embellished with cream cheese and pimento and stabbed meatballs with skewers. Laurel smiled to herself and remembered her thoughts at the Cavanaugh Thanksgiving. If she'd magically stepped into a movie, what might it be called? *A Very Spencer Holiday* or perhaps *A Rocky Mountain Christmas Miracle*. Maybe holiday movies weren't as far from real life as she'd assumed. She'd never known a similar Christmas, but apparently others had. The Cavanaughs, for example, likely stirred hot chocolate with peppermint sticks and threw snowballs at each other when they went to cut down their Christmas tree.

That thought prompted her to go look at the variety of trees and decorations in the center of the immense high-ceilinged room. She was enthralled by the handmade creations of glass, felt, wood and paper mâché on each unique tree. She certainly wouldn't be making her own ornaments, but she decided to buy a tree to decorate. She put several ornaments in a small basket and paid the young man who offered to help her. He wrapped them carefully and placed them in a box.

Laurel retrieved her coat and carried her purchase to the car with a feeling of accomplishment. It had started snowing while she'd been inside, and her feet were freezing by the time she got to her car. She used her neck scarf to brush the snow from her pumps. She would have to remember to put a pair of winter boots in her trunk.

The snow was falling more heavily as she headed along Highway 34, and she drove slowly with her high beams only reflecting white flurries. Turning onto her driveway was questionable, but there was an open area with no weeds or brush, so she aimed for that. She immediately knew she'd chosen wrong when the front right side of her car sunk downward.

She'd felt so good about herself this evening. Of course, something like this had to happen. She could get out and hobble the considerable length of the drive to the house and wait until morning. But depending on the amount of snow that fell, waiting might make it worse. Should she call a tow truck? She was right here at her house.

She tried backing out of the drainage ditch, but the front tire only spun.

Mariah Carey's high notes on *All I Want for Christmas is You* had never been so irritating. She punched off the music and drummed her fingers on the steering wheel.

At a glare of light across her car's interior, she turned to spot the vehicle traveling the highway. A truck by the size of it. The vehicle slowed, the driver steering to her side of the road and stopping. A person emerged from each side of the cab. One tall and broad, the other much smaller. She rolled down her window.

"Laurel? Are you all right?" Unmistakably Joe's voice.

The two approached her car. She opened her door and got out.

"Your hair is so pretty." Chloe looked down. "You're wearing heels in the snow."

"Yes," she answered. "I was unprepared for this."

"Are you all right?" Joe asked again.

"Feeling foolish never killed anyone," she answered.

"Don't feel bad. It happens all the time out here. I should have noticed the reflectors were gone. There should be several on each side of the drive. That's on me."

"You're hardly to blame," she disagreed.

"Get back in. Chloe, you get in with her. I'll hook a tow chain and pull you back. Make sure it's in neutral until you're out. Then you can drive forward."

Chloe got in the driver's side first and slid over to the

passenger seat. Laurel slid in behind her and turned up the heat.

"Good thing we were just coming home," Chloe said.

"I really didn't know what I was going to do. Oh, my gosh, does he have to get under the car?"

"If you don't have a tow hitch, he has to hook it to an axle or something. He'll be fine. He's done it a million times."

Laurel watched as Joe reappeared covered in snow, brushed himself off and went back to his truck to attach the chain. A few minutes later, he'd pulled her car out of the ditch and unhooked the chain. He knocked on her back window, indicating she should drive forward.

She pulled under the carport beside her cabin and she and Chloe got out. Joe had parked behind her and joined them.

"Here." He grasped her arm through her coat and helped her walk to the door.

"You two come in and get warm," she said. "I'll start a fire and make something hot to drink."

"I'll start the fire," he offered.

They all brushed snow from their clothing and entered the cabin. Laurel flipped on lights. "I bought a grill lighter. It's on the mantle."

"This is nice." Chloe handed Laurel her coat and Laurel hung all three on backs of dining chairs. "You have so many pretty things. Dad, look at her throw pillows. We're going to need some of these."

He glanced up from stacking wood on the grate. "We're going to need a lot of things."

"Oh, your outfit is crazy sick," Chloe declared. "You are lit."

Laurel glanced at Joe.

He only smiled and picked up the lighter.

"Thank you, Chloe." Laurel removed her wet shoes and went for a pair of warm socks.

"Did you have a date?" Chloe asked when she returned.

"No, I went to the fundraiser Christmas party at the artists' co-op. It was nice. I had a good time and met people."

"I'll bet you were the prettiest one there," Chloe said.

"I guarantee it," her dad replied without looking up.

His compliment warmed her more than the fire ever could. His admiration was puzzling, but a heady pleasure. "Would you rather have coffee or hot chocolate?" Laurel asked. "I only have the instant kind of chocolate mix. I do have wine though."

He looked at her then. "I'll take the coffee. Night like this, I might get called out."

Chloe accompanied her to the kitchen, where Laurel made a mug of hot chocolate and two cups of coffee.

"You know, if your dad's ever gone and you want company, you can always come over here." She handed Chloe her mug.

"Thanks. I always know I can call Grandma, but it's good to know you're here too."

Joe had the fire going when they returned, and the three of them sat in front of the hearth with their hot drinks.

Laurel extended her socked feet toward the fire. "I'll put my winter boots in my car and order another pair," she said. "That won't happen again."

"I'll grab some reflectors tomorrow," Joe assured her. "I feel bad about that. You obviously weren't going fast, but you could have gotten banged up." He turned to his daughter. "And no, I don't have a hero complex."

Chloe laughed. "I always tell him that because he's always helping people."

"Someone with a hero or a savior complex has to be the only one saving people," Laurel told her. "Sometimes to the detriment of others. I think your dad is just a nice guy. Plus, it's his job to help people."

Joe inclined his head toward her, "Thank you."

"How do you know this stuff?" Chloe asked.

Laurel sipped her coffee. "I read a lot."

"What's Peter Pan syndrome?"

Surprised by the question, Laurel raised her eyebrows. "It's when someone doesn't consider themselves an adult and usually doesn't hold down a permanent job. They might be kind of a dreamer and blame their failures on other people."

"Well, then that's not Uncle Crosby at all," Chloe said. "Aunt Brooke and Aunt Steph always say that about him."

"No, it's not him at all. They're teasing him like little sisters do," Joe told her. "Your Uncle Crosby has his own business and lived in his own home until Grandpa died. He wanted to be there for Grandma, so he rented out his house and moved in with her."

"He just has a lot of different girlfriends," Chloe said.

Joe agreed with a purse of his lips. "That he does. I'd call them dates, though. Girlfriend implies a relationship."

Chloe wrinkled her nose. "What's up with that?"

"That I do not know," he answered.

Laurel glanced at Joe. "Families are sure up in your business, aren't they? Does that ever bother you?"

Joe chuckled. "Sometimes it does. You should have heard the flack I took for selling a perfectly good house in town and building out here on the lake. And when I moved us into the Airstream, you'd have thought I left Chloe out for the crows to pick her bones."

Chloe giggled at that.

"It's not like I didn't present it to her and give her a say in the decision. She's getting tired of living life cramped, but I know she still shares the dream with me."

"Oh, Dad, you're so corny."

"Am I wrong?"

"No. It's going to be super cool when we get moved in and I have a huge bedroom and all my stuff. I get a new bed. And sleepovers." She got up and sat on the sofa. "I was at one at my friend Becca's last night, so I'm zonked. Can I lay my head on this pillow?"

"Of course," Laurel answered. "I can get you a more comfortable one if you like."

"Don't get up. This is fine. Can I use this fluffy throw?"

"Yes, of course."

Chloe pulled the woven blanket over herself and snuggled in comfortably.

Laurel exchanged a smile with Joe.

Watching the two of them interact fascinated her. She'd never had the opportunity to see a father and daughter in a close personal setting. She'd seen others while shopping and occasionally observed children and parents on the street. Listening to their conversations, watching their expressions, everything about them was artlessly intimate. They didn't measure their words or gauge each other's expressions. She'd noticed the same familiarity at the Cavanaugh's huge Thanksgiving dinner.

"Tell me about the fancy shindig," he said, checking her thoughts.

She told him about the music and the wonderful smells and about who she'd met.

"Whitney Chandler is in town? Is that still her name?"

"I think so. I don't recall hearing a different name."

"I went to school with her and Matt. Their folks had a place where the college campus is now. Their mother still lives in Spencer."

"Whitney seemed like a very smart, very accomplished person. She's a curator for a textile museum in Idaho."

"You find people interesting, don't you?"

"I guess so," she said. "Why do you ask?"

"I don't know. I've seen you watching people like you're learning something."

"I didn't realize I did that."

"Everyone does to an extent. But you seem fascinated.

And you were able to answer Chloe's questions about psychological things. Have you studied psychology? I took a few courses for my criminal law degree."

"Some," she answered. "Not that many courses. The fact is I've worked with quite a few psychologists and therapists."

"As in you've done their websites?"

She was leaning back against a chair and brought her knees up and wrapped her arms around them. "No. As in going to them for treatment."

"Oh. Sorry. I didn't mean to pry."

She straightened her legs and reached a hand over to his shoulder. "No, it's okay. I wouldn't answer if I didn't want to." She turned and glanced at Chloe, who was now sleeping soundly. "I know it's ironic. I'm a social media manager with social anxiety."

He acknowledged that with a nod. "I don't know anything about that."

"Well, it's more common than you might think. A specific type would be fear of public speaking. But someone like me with a general anxiety disorder is uncomfortable in all social situations. I've been working for years to overcome this, and I'm much improved."

"You must be if you went to that party tonight. Fancy parties make me uncomfortable."

"And you're a people person."

"Am I?"

She gave him a soft smile. "Yes." She sipped her coffee and set the mug on the floor. "My therapist assigned me a series of exercises I'm working my way through."

"Do you want to tell me what they are?"

"The first one was the easiest. Talk to the mail carrier, the cashier at the grocery, the bank teller. Make eye contact. It's not like I've never talked to people. I went to college and had job interviews. I've talked to people." She smoothed the hem of her emerald green skirt between her thumb and forefinger. "It's easier not to, however, and it's a constant, almost urgent temptation not to huddle in on myself."

He didn't remark on her words, seemed to be simply listening.

"Some of the steps are harder, like saying yes to invitations."

"Invitations like Thanksgiving dinner?"

She observed him under her lashes. "I found out that saying yes can be a really good thing."

He grinned, glanced at Chloe, then back at her.

"I've never thought of myself as a normal person," she admitted. "I've missed out on doing things that normal people do."

"What kinds of things?"

She gestured with an open palm. "A family dinner." She rested her fingertips on her breastbone. "I don't have a family." Lowering her hand, she went on. "Normal things others do, like learn to play a guitar or roller skating or skeet shooting."

"Skeet shooting?"

"They do it in the movies."

He nodded. "Okay."

"Drive a go cart," she added, then touched her skirt. "Wear a fancy party dress."

Joe had been admiring her striking coloring in the clothing she was wearing. He imagined her in that setting at the Old Stone Church. She'd undoubtedly been the most beautiful woman there. But she hadn't cared that her hair got wet outdoors or that she might not look fashionable wearing her bulky socks with her skirt. He appreciated her lack of vanity. "You sure look pretty in that green skirt and your little black top."

"Thank you."

The fire crackled and a spark flew against the inside of the screen, then burned out.

"I had a bad dream the night before going to dinner at your mother's." She described a dream about the mangy dog, and how she'd been afraid it was going to hurt him. "When we got to her house, it was like a carnival. Your mother didn't look anything like she actually looks, and she didn't like me at all."

"Sometimes it is like a carnival, but my mom definitely likes you."

"It doesn't take a genius to figure out the dream was all about my groundless fears that something terrible is going to happen. The dread has been disabling me for years. But then…" She opened both hands and dropped them to her lap. "Nothing terrible happened. My fears are unfounded, which is what I'm supposed to be learning."

"That's good." He ran a hand over his jaw. She'd disclosed a little more about her life growing up and her education but had never mentioned anything personal. He couldn't get past his concern that she spent a lot of energy trying to avoid attention. "What about other relationships?"

She raised her deep brown eyes to his, and he couldn't read her reaction. "Like romantic relationships?"

"Yes. Boyfriends. A husband?"

She glanced away. "No. Nothing like that."

It was nearly impossible to believe she'd lived her life without a romantic entanglement. He picked up his mug and reached for her hand.

She stood with his help, got her mug and Chloe's and followed him to the kitchen, where they set them in the sink.

"You know I was married to Chloe's mother." Chloe's mother wasn't someone he talked about, because everyone in Spencer already knew he'd once been married. They didn't know all the details, but they knew enough. Maybe if he shared something, Laurel would be more comfortable. "We weren't married that long. I'd graduated college, recently become a deputy and worked crazy hours. I didn't realize she wasn't happy when she got pregnant. She quit her job and stayed home. Didn't clean the house or cook. Didn't do much of anything except pick fights when I got home, no matter the hour."

Laurel leaned back against the counter and listened.

"I thought it was hormones or whatever and that after the baby came, she'd snap out of it. She wouldn't hear of counseling. When Chloe was born, I fell in love with that tiny helpless little girl." He cleared his throat. "Shelby resented having the responsibility and hated staying home. She took care of herself, but left Chloe with my mom a lot. She was drinking more than I knew at the time. Let me take care of Chloe. After a few weeks, she packed her things and told me she was done. She didn't want to be a mother or a wife. And she left."

"That must have been terrible for you," Laurel said.

"It was. My mom helped. Colette helped. Between us we managed to raise her."

"No wonder Chloe is so close to all of them. And to Avery and Kyle."

He nodded.

"And she gave you custody."

"I went after sole custody and insisted," he answered. "I respect it if you don't want to share personal things like that. I don't talk about my past either."

She studied him. "I've honestly never had a relationship like a steady boyfriend or a husband. I didn't date in college. I had a study friend, and that was the closest I've ever been to what I'd call a relationship."

"A guy friend?"

"Yes. We were both focused on studies. It wasn't romantic." She leaned toward him, looking into his eyes. "What about you? Girlfriends in Spencer since your wife?"

"Dates here and there. I saw one person for a year or so,

but when Chloe was small, my schedule didn't give me much time to devote away from her."

"Where is she now?"

"Married with kids."

Laurel leaned back against the counter.

He took a step closer and placed his hands on her shoulders. She felt so small and fragile beneath his touch. This woman *was* fragile, and he had to remember that. She was either incredibly inexperienced or a really good liar and hiding from someone. She seemed too sincere to be lying. If she was withholding something, the fact wouldn't shock him, though. Especially if she felt her safety was at risk.

When she looked up at him, crazy things happened in his chest. He wasn't a teenager, so his reactions discomfited him. He wasn't used to feeling unnerved in any situation.

She raised a hand to flatten her palm on his chest, and she surely must have felt the increased rate of his heart.

He rested his hand over hers. "It's not skeet shooting, but is more kissing on your bucket list?"

CHAPTER TEN

*H*er cheeks pinkened charmingly. "Admittedly, yes."

He leaned forward at the same time she raised her face, and their lips met. Not quite as tenderly as the first time, but every bit as earnestly. Quite naturally, she folded against him, wrapping her arms around his back to spread her hands flat. Oh, she felt incredibly good in his arms, soft and yet resilient. Her heart raced against his chest. He didn't want to regret this, but he hadn't felt this way about a woman for a long time, maybe never.

He ran his palms down her sleek slender arms and back up. She shivered beneath his touch. Though she seemed delicate, her bones, her skin...everything he knew about her told him she was strong and determined. She was fragile emotionally, as well, having been orphaned and shuffled around in foster care.

Joe lifted both hands to frame her face and thread his fingers into her dark tresses. He inched away. Her expressive dark eyes were luminous and wide, as though questioning.

He wanted to make her feel safe, wanted her to be

comfortable and trust him, though he wasn't sure why that need was so important. He kissed her again in a series of soft touches bestowed on her lips. "Does this scare you?" he asked.

"A little." Her reply came out on a breath. She quickly raised her hands to his upper arms and held him fast. "I'm not afraid of you, Joe. It's…well, it's that I'm afraid of things that make me feel vulnerable."

Concerned then that he was leaning against her, he turned them around, so that his back was against the counter and she leaned her weight into him. "So, you're afraid of what you're feeling…or that letting yourself feel is risky?"

"Yes, that's it exactly." She reached to stroke her fingertips over his jaw, resting one in a spot where he had a small scar. "What happened here?"

"Dirt bike accident when I was twelve. It looked pretty cool for a while."

She smiled.

"Nothing bad is going to happen to you when you're with me," he told her.

"I believe that." She rested her head against his chest then, and he gently rested a hand over the back of her head.

She felt so good in his arms.

Uneasy guilt gripped his conscience, a bolt of fear following right behind. He couldn't expect her to be open with him if he held back with her, but this was something he'd never admitted to anyone, and had trouble admitting to himself. His crazy heart beat even faster. "There's something I've never told anyone."

"No one?"

He grimaced. "No. It's something humiliating."

Her dark eyes were wide and shining as she looked into his. He might regret it if he told her, but he would definitely regret it if he didn't. "I told you I was shot in the knee."

"You did."

"I didn't tell you how it happened."

"I assumed you were involved in something on the job."

"Not exactly."

"I only ever told one person the truth, and that person took responsibility for not revealing all the facts."

"What happened?"

"My wife shot me."

Her body reacted and he felt it. "What?"

"I stopped home on a night close to the Fourth of July, and she'd been drinking. A lot. Chloe was in the house with her, asleep in her crib, but if something had happened, Shelby couldn't have taken care of her. I was furious, and we fought. I told her I was taking Chloe somewhere safe, and she freaked out, yelling that baby was all I ever cared about."

Laurel took a deep breath as she listened wide-eyed.

"I never saw it coming. She reached between the sofa cushions and pulled out a revolver. I'm trained for assaults and deadly situations, so I didn't try to grab for it, which could have been disastrous. I backed away and gave her space. Talked to her. She waved that gun around—I don't think she intended to actually shoot it. She was beyond reasoning with though, too drunk to be coherent, and she pulled the trigger."

"Oh, Joe, that's awful. What happened?"

"There were fireworks going off outside, and no one thought anything of another loud pop in the neighborhood. I went down, but I got up and grabbed the gun from her. I got Chloe, went out and got in my vehicle and made two phone calls. The first was to my mom. I told her there was a problem with Shelby and to come down to the curb and take Chloe from me while I was on my lunch hour. I dropped her off at my folks'.

"The second call?"

"To my boss, the former sheriff, Atwood Tanner. I didn't use the radio. I called him on my phone. I told him what had happened."

"What happened then?"

"He told me not to say anything to anyone and to let him do the talking. He asked if I could drive and told me to meet him at the ER. He met me there and walked me in. He told them I'd been shot by a drunk waving a gun around. The team looked at the wound, gave me something for pain, and when I woke up, Atwood was sitting beside me. They'd given him the bullet they took out of my leg."

"What did he do?"

"Nothing." He took a breath. "He never wrote a report. I questioned him about it, but he said I didn't need something like a domestic dispute in my file. I didn't realize he had his eye on me all along for his replacement. He told me it was his decision and he'd live with it. He's the one person who knows the truth."

"Until me."

"Until you. Atwood is my deputy Jericho's dad. He said he was going to make sure Shelby got help, and I think he might have gone to talk to her that night or the next day. But she didn't get help. She just packed up and took off. It was over."

"Of course, you didn't want anyone to know," Laurel said. "You didn't want Chloe to know what had happened."

"I'd have been the deputy whose own wife shot him, but he spared me that."

Resting her hand over his heart, she said, "I'll never say a word to anyone."

"I know you won't." He'd already figured out she was good at keeping secrets.

She hugged him, and he was glad he'd told her. He felt something intense and meaningful for this woman, and holding back part of himself wouldn't have been as real as he wanted this relationship to be.

Over her shoulder, he glanced at a small desk area built into the wall beside her two-person table. A couple of books and a tablet lay there beside a coffee mug holding pens and pencils. On the wall above the desk hung a calendar with several sticky notes attached, reminding him of something.

He straightened, taking her with him, until they stood apart. "My department has a couple of Christmas parties in order to accommodate both shifts. I was wondering if you'd like to join me. We have dinner and then go to the Wild Card for drinks. "It's a nice upscale dinner in Olde Town. The steaks are great, the seafood is flown in fresh. Good wine." He raised an eyebrow. "On the county's tab."

She seemed to think it over for a brief moment before nodding. "That sounds nice."

"I hope that wasn't unfair. I mean, since you're being coached to say yes instead of no."

"I wouldn't say yes if I didn't want to."

"Great."

She stepped aside and reached to get their mugs and put them into the dishwasher.

As she did that, he glanced again at her calendar, getting a closer look. A pink sticky note read:

Jim
Dec 15th / 10am
Brookside Café

The Brookside Café was in downtown Denver, one of the city's top-rated breakfast cafes. That was a long way to travel during the winter for breakfast, so obviously the person she was meeting was important—or the meeting was important.

Who was Jim? Granted, he hadn't known her long, but she'd said she had no family.

"I'd better wake Chloe and get her home."

She dried her hands on a towel. "Thank you for coming to my rescue tonight. And thank you...for everything."

"I'm your man." He rethought that statement. "I mean, you know...any time. I'm here to help you out."

She gave him a soft smile. "I know."

Back in the living room, he gently woke Chloe and helped her get into her coat and boots. She gave Laurel a hug, and he escorted his daughter out to the truck.

The snow had stopped falling and was already slush on the highway. He parked and ushered Chloe into the Airstream, where she gave him a sleepy-eyed peck on the cheek and went to her room.

Joe drank a glass of milk, grabbed a book he'd been reading, and stretched out on the sofa. He couldn't focus on the words because he couldn't get Laurel's date with Jim out of his head. He could have asked. Why didn't he just ask?

Because that was being nosy. Maybe because he was afraid she'd lie to him.

Was it any of his business? He hadn't been able to find anything suspicious in her past and no reports of abuse or restraining orders, but his searches had been glaringly missing the first twenty-some years of her life—enough to make him question why. Could this Jim be a problem for her? If she was afraid of someone, if she was running, which seemed likely, maybe it *was* his business.

Could Jim be a problem for the lodge? She was now working for a man and a company for whom many things could be a security risk. Politicians and all kinds of public figures stayed at Aspen Gold Lodge. It was his job to keep the community safe, to investigate or report anything that he deemed suspicious. Snipers and assassins did stuff like befriending innocents to get close to a target all the time. If he was going to err, he intended to err on the side of caution.

Maybe justifying checking out this guy was a good excuse to learn about Jim.

And he wanted to know who Jim was.

❧

"I have a job for you." Joe spoke to the investigator he'd used on several occasions. This guy had tracked down his ex-wife so Joe could have divorce and custody papers served, and Joe had called him for work issues several times over the years. He didn't have the same agencies at his fingertips that Jakob Spencer's security team did, but because of his position, he had plenty of resources.

Joe gave him the time and place. "I need photos so I can ID the man."

"You've got it. Breakfast on you at the Brookside Café sounds good to me."

Joe didn't have to bother with a mention of discretion. This guy was a pro. No one would know they'd been observed or photographed.

By that weekend, the cabin had been completely framed, sided and roofed, and the HVAC and plumbing and electricity had been installed. He'd been able to work inside now that the was weather was cold. The great room had a vaulted ceiling with reclaimed finished lumber, and Crosby had helped him build an enormous stone fireplace. The mantle and flanking cabinets bore live edges. He'd gotten as far as installing drywall in a few rooms, and purchasing cabinets and sink for the kitchen, but the materials were stacked everywhere. Crosby had promised to come and bring a friend that morning.

Joe couldn't have been more surprised when cars started pulling up his drive and family members and friends spilled out. His mom and Colette carried in coolers and insulated dishes. "I promised everyone lasagna if they showed up to work," his mom said. Tyler carried in the six-foot tables and folding chairs always stored in his mom's garage. Dusty and Kendra arrived, as well as both of his sisters, and he got the biggest kick out of Stephanie in spotless new overalls, work boots, and a crisp white shirt with the cuffs rolled back.

"You made the *Vogue* handyman edition?" he asked.

She punched him in the arm. "Dusty has a toolbelt for me too."

"Louis Vuitton makes tool belts now?" Brooke asked, coming in behind her wearing old faded jeans and a flannel shirt. She carried a huge plastic barrel cooler to serve drinks from, obviously not full. You have running water, right?"

"Yep. But not in the kitchen yet. I was hoping to put up cupboards today and get the sink installed. I thought only Crosby was coming."

"Surprise. He made it a family day." Brooke set down the cooler and gave him a robust hug. "Love you, big brother."

Joe got a catch in his throat at her expression of affection. She'd always been a hugger, always told people she loved them. That was one of the things he appreciated most about her. He kissed the top of her head and lifted her off the ground in a bear-hug. "Love you, little sister."

She pushed away. "What do you want me to do?"

"You can peel the stickers off all the windows and clean them. You can vacuum out the sills. If the glass gets covered with drywall dust later, we can vacuum that off."

"Do you have a razor blade scraper? Oh, here." Brooke took window cleaner and rags from one of the boxes of supplies along the wall. "Ten-four."

Crosby showed up with Keane Dalgleish, one of the brothers who ran a construction company in town. He did the bids and helped organize crews. From his left knee down, he wore a prosthetic, but Joe had never seen the fact stop him from doing anything. He and Crosby had even snow skied with the brothers a few times.

Joe grinned and reached to shake Keane's hand. "My little brother brought the pro today?"

Keane grinned good-naturedly. "I don't get enough of this during the week, apparently. Dusty thought we'd be drywalling, so I brought my own stilts."

"You're a good man," Joe told him. "You will be rewarded, of course. My mom and sister brought food."

"Yes!" Keane said with a fist bump.

Barney managed to get inside with the next volunteers who entered the house and went straight to Ian. When the big yellow lab licked his face, Ian giggled and swiped his sleeve over his chin and lips.

"Barney, no kisses," Joe said in a stern voice.

The dog sat up straight with his tail smacking the subflooring, looking from Ian to Joe.

"Good boy," Joe said.

Enough family and friends showed up to divide into work teams. While drywall was going up in the bedrooms, others hung kitchen cupboards to Joe's specifications. He'd already hung and finished that drywall himself.

Having this help was going to move the progress forward in a vast leap. Joe had known building his own cabin would be a huge undertaking, and he'd been all in for the work, but the myriad of details had become burdensome, and Chloe deserved to get into a house and be comfortable.

As the noon hour rolled around, Liz and her daughters and daughter-in-law conferred and realized no one had brought forks.

"We only have four in the Airstream," Joe told her.

"My fault. I'll just run and get plastic," Liz said.

"Grandma, that's a long way into town," Chloe said. "I'll just go over and borrow forks from Laurel."

"Invite her to come for lunch!" Liz called after her.

"And tell her to put on work clothes," Brooke called.

His mother stood beside him as Joe opened a box of wood screws and filled a pouch on his tool belt. "Anything serious going on there?"

She understood him well, and knew his struggle after Shelby had left. He'd rarely dated in fifteen years, and he'd never had another real relationship. "I don't know if it's serious," he answered honestly. "It's something, but I don't know that she's a person who can be all in."

And that was what he'd require if ever he was to fall in love with someone. He would require honesty and whole-hearted commitment.

She patted his arm. "You'll know if it's right."

❦

Laurel changed into jeans and a t-shirt, grabbed her coat and pulled on boots. She walked with Chloe through the wooded area between her house and Joe's Airstream. Approaching the new cabin was the first time she'd seen the structure up close. The house was huge from the front, two stories, with enormous dormers and multi-paned windows. A stone chimney matched the rock that trimmed the walkway. She hadn't been prepared for the open concept inside, however. Two-story windows the entire width of a great room looked out over Twin Owl Lake and let all that glorious reflected light indoors.

Half a dozen people greeted her at once, dividing her attention between the breathtaking view and their warm welcome.

"Oh, my goodness," she breathed.

"It's something, isn't it?" Kendra asked from beside her. "Dusty actually suggested tearing down my Aunt Sophie's house—well it's my house now—and building something like this. I said absolutely not, of course. My whole childhood is wrapped up in that house."

"The house with the red roof on the other side of where I'm renting?"

"Yes, it was my aunt's home and the only safe homey place I ever knew until I knew the Cavanaughs. We're renting it out now, but we plan to reserve a month for ourselves every summer to come stay and fish."

"I don't blame you. I've never fished, but I enjoy sitting on the deck when the weather permits."

"Next summer I'll come get you to go fishing with me."

"You go out on the lake alone?" Laurel asked.

Kendra nodded. "Often. It's like…meditation."

Laurel smiled.

"Everyone come dig in," Liz called. "There's water, hand soap and paper towels in the hall bathroom to wash up."

Colette showed up with clean hands and face, but her t-shirt caked with grayish clay-looking fingerprints. "Hey, Laurel. Thanks for saving the day with forks."

"Not a problem," she replied. "What's your task?"

"I spread drywall compound in the joints and Dusty comes behind me and smooths it out. We have a bedroom finished and are waiting for it to dry."

Everyone quite naturally congregated in the great room, which didn't have its hardwood flooring yet, and a few had chairs, but most sat on buckets, coolers and their rolled-up sweatshirts, balancing sturdy disposable plates on their laps. Laurel sat on the floor, and a minute later Joe joined her. "Hey, thanks for the forks."

"I didn't really earn my lunch," she said.

"You're welcome to stick around this afternoon."

"Okay. Someone will have to show me what to do."

He grinned and stabbed a bite of lasagna. "Never a problem with this bunch. They love to tell people what to do."

"Joe, this house is incredible. That view nearly stopped my heart."

He glanced from her to the windows. "It's something, isn't it? It's what I always envisioned, and here it is. The place is a long way from finished, but one of these days I'll sit here in comfort and look out over that lake. I can have everyone over for holidays. Someday even Chloe's kids."

She envied his dream and his life with family, always assured of them, confident of his place in their midst. "That must be a good feeling."

Joe studied her for a moment and then averted his attention to the others who'd taken spots on the floor nearby. "Laurel, this is Keane. He's the pro here. His family has a construction company."

"Hi, Laurel," Keane said with a friendly nod.

"And this is my deputy, Jericho Tanner."

"What a great name," she told the good-looking guy who might have been thirty.

"I have a sister named Bethel and a brother named Judah. I always thought I came out the winner."

"They're places in the Bible, right? Is your family in the ministry?"

He chuckled. "My dad's the retired sheriff."

His dad was Joe's former boss. The man he'd told her knew what happened in his past. He glanced at her, and she met his eyes.

They had a secret.

Another day and she'd be meeting a man named Jim in Denver. Maybe after that he'd have more insight into facts about her. The things she said didn't match up with the things she did. She'd told him she had no friends or family, hadn't been in a relationship, but she was meeting someone.

Still, he didn't regret telling her. It had been the right thing to do.

After lunch, Laurel and Chloe were the clean-up detail,

which neither minded. They filled a trash bag with all the used plates, and Laurel placed all of the forks in a plastic bag to wash at home later.

Chloe leaned in close. "Do you know who Audrey Knox is?"

"The singer on the cover of half the magazines in the checkout lanes?"

"Yeah, that's her."

"Yes, I know who she is."

"Did you know she's from Spencer?"

Laurel held open another trash bag while Chloe tossed in empty water bottles to recycle. "No way. I don't pay much attention to those magazines, but are you serious?"

"You wouldn't learn it in a magazine. Celebrities keep a low profile for good reasons."

"I'm sure that's true," Laurel replied.

"Well, she and Jericho were a thing in high school. They played together at the fairs and summer concerts."

Laurel widened her eyes.

"Then she went to Nashville and had her first hit song."

Laurel ran the news through her memory. "*Maybe I'm the One?*"

"That's it. She got famous and married her manager and only comes back once in a while to see her mom."

"Get out of town."

"No, for real. See, when you're born in Spencer, you learn that this town is all about tourists. The town grew around the lodge and because of location became a great place to visit. The tourists, like they support everything—the lodge, the shops and small businesses."

Laurel left the bag open for later and rested it against a wall. "The economy, yes."

"Famous people visit Spencer a lot. It's our...I guess you'd say *culture*...but there's a rule we learn—if we see someone famous, we don't ask for an autograph or take photos or anything like that. It's rude to bother them or point them out. They pay big bucks for privacy at the lodge, and sometimes they come into town."

"It makes sense that everyone knows and accepts that," Laurel said thoughtfully. "It's respectful."

"I never know who the old people are," Chloe continued. "I heard Harrison Ford was here before, and Michael Keaton. I probably pass people and don't recognize them, but if like Nick Jonas was at the skating rink or something, I'd freak out."

Laurel laughed. "I would too."

"Is he your favorite?"

"No, Joe's my favorite."

Chloe laughed at that. "Figures. It's the name?"

Laurel shook her head and tied the trash bag shut. "Audrey Knox is gorgeous and talented, and to think I might see her by accident someday."

"Sometimes she still sings at the fair."

"I had no idea. Wouldn't that be fun?"

"The Rockwell County Fairgrounds has an awesome event center. If she does a concert here, let's go together.

Laurel closed the lids on the coolers. "Absolutely. Who is assigning tasks today?"

"We'll ask Dad or Uncle Crosby."

They got the job of cleaning a bathroom that had recently been drywalled and grouted. Laurel had never spent time around a teenager. She already enjoyed Chloe, but getting to know her as they worked was even more enjoyable. It felt good to be part of something, to participate in a community workday

"You've done this sort of thing before? Worked with family and friends on a project?" she asked.

Chloe rolled her eyes. "Ever since I was little. Just like Ian, sometimes you play around, but the adults give you lots of jobs. A couple months ago, everyone painted the inside and outside of Uncle Dusty and Aunt Kendra's house before they moved in. Uncle Crosby landscaped it, and I was lucky 'cause I got to help him with trees and plants and stuff."

"It'll be a while before you can do that here," Laurel said. "Spring, I suppose."

"That'll be cool. I just want the inside done, so we can move in."

"Show me which room is yours."

Chloe led her to a large bedroom with its own bathroom on the second floor, where Brooke and Colette were painting. The windows and woodwork had been taped over with blue painter's tape. Colette trimmed around the windows with a brush and Brooke was rolling on a luscious lavender color. A wide dormer held double windows that looked out over the lake, and beneath the windows a frame for a bench had been constructed.

"This was the first room where Dad put up the walls," Chloe said with a smile. "He knew how much I wanted to see it get finished."

Hammering from more than once source echoed from other rooms.

"Kyle and Avery helped with your closet, but they've moved on to another room with Tyler and Dusty," Brooke said. "I think they're putting shelves in your dad's closet now."

Chloe opened the closet door and squealed. "This is lit!"

Laurel joined her to find it was a walk-in closet. Drawers and shelves had been built in with enough space in the center for a bench or chair. "Oh, my goodness. This closet looks like it's from a magazine."

"I showed him a picture of a closet I liked, and this is almost exactly like it." Chloe grabbed Laurel's hands and jumped up and down with delight. "He's the best dad ever! I have to go tell Dad I love it!" She ran from the closet and out of the bedroom.

Grinning, Laurel watched her go and went back to where the two women were working. "That's a happy kid there."

"She deserves it," Brooke said.

Laurel remembered what Joe had told her about how these two had helped his mom take care of Chloe when she was a baby. She'd thought the saying about taking a village to raise a child had only been a cliché, but this family had proven it true—and were raising some pretty great kids.

"I'd better get back to my job," Laurel said. "I don't want to get fired on my first day."

"Don't count on it. No one has ever been able to get fired," Brooke called after her.

Supper was pizza delivery, with another easy clean-up. A couple of helpers left, but a few more arrived to work through the evening. Laurel met Matt Chandler, the outfitter, Dan Rivers, a paramedic, and Levi Ephram, a police officer.

A lot of weary men and women left Joe's in the dark that night. All the while Joe walked her home, she marveled at the sense of accomplishment buoying her. His home was a lot nearer to completion because of the effort of all those people, and she'd worked alongside them throughout the day. No one had seemed to think it was odd that she was part of the assembly of helpers. No one had asked her prying questions or given her curious looks.

When Joe told her goodnight and thanked her, she said, "It was a pleasure," and she meant it. He'd been in a hurry to get back to the Airstream and shower, so she hadn't invited him in. The day, their parting, all of it had felt comfortable.

She'd been present in the day, and it had been wonderful. That took care of step five on her list of exercises, and it hadn't even been deliberate. She would have so much to tell Dr. Easton at her appointment on Tuesday. None of the things she'd done recently had been a struggle. She'd almost forgotten about her list. For the first time she could remember, Laurel was experiencing a sense of peace. Spencer, these people, her progress, all of it was adding up to a monumental realization....

She fit in.

She felt normal.

These people, today, this town—were all what home felt like.

CHAPTER ELEVEN

$\mathcal{L}$aurel found a spot in the parking garage and walked into the Brookside Café in midtown Denver. "I'm meeting someone," she told the hostess while glancing toward the booths. "I see him."

Jim Denning got up from where he'd been sipping a cup of coffee and greeted her. "You look great."

He waited for her to move first and then enclosed her in a brief hug.

"Thanks," she said. "It's so good to see you."

They seated themselves across from one another and both took long assessing looks. He looked another year older, but still had a face she couldn't get enough of. His thick hair was completely silver now, which always caught her by surprise, because the image of a tall, strong, brown-haired man was permanently imbedded in her memory.

"So, you're living in Spencer," he said.

"I am. I can't wait to tell you this." She first took stock of the interior of the restaurant, noticed who was sitting nearby, who occupied the other booths, then leaned forward. "I got a contract with the Aspen Gold Lodge. It's the biggest client I've ever taken on, and I'm completely up for it. I got a signing check and paid off the rest of my student loans and have savings."

A server brought them water and set a coffee cup in front of Laurel. "Coffee?"

"Yes, thanks." After the woman had poured and walked away, Laurel finished telling him about the job.

"Did you find a therapist there that you like?" he asked.

The server took their orders, and Laurel was still telling her old friend about what had been happening as they ate. Thirty minutes later, she finally stopped talking. "I haven't let you get a word in edgewise."

He lifted a hand from the table and made a negative motion. "I've never heard you this excited about a place or… well, about anything."

"I've never been this enthused, and I've definitely never felt as healthy. It's like…" She paused a moment. "I feel normal with these people. Of course, they don't know me or who I am, but I'm a new person with them."

"With the sheriff?" he asked pointedly.

She'd known this man since she'd been ten years old. He'd saved her life. Literally. He wasn't family, but he was the only person who really knew her.

She nodded easily. "With Joe."

"I'm really happy for you," he said. "This day has been a long time coming. You've come so far from that little girl I first laid eyes on."

Laurel reached over and laid her hand over his on the tabletop. "I owe you my life. A lot of it has been pretty dysfunctional and some downright miserable, but I wouldn't be here today if it hadn't been for you. I would never have had this chance at finding something real. I'll never be able to thank you like you deserve."

"You were a terrified ten-year-old when I found you in that shed," he said, his voice gruff. "I did what anyone would have done."

She shook her head. "Not the person who left me there."

"Dying in prison was too good for him," he replied. "Seeing you like this is one of the best days of my life."

"Tell me what you've been doing," she urged. His wife had endured a lengthy illness before passing away a few years ago, and he'd been traveling off and on since then. They checked in with each other every couple of months and met up somewhere once or twice a year.

The lunch crowd was filtering in when they finally wound up their conversation and stood to leave. Jim had picked up the ticket, as usual, but she left the server a hefty tip, since she'd refilled their coffee cups half a dozen times. Laurel's oldest friend walked her to her car in the parking garage, and she gave him a sound hug.

"It means so much to me to see you happy," he said. "Think you'll still be in Colorado next summer?"

"I hope so." She thought a second and corrected her reply. "I think so."

He nodded. "We'll meet then."

"It's a date." Heart full, she watched him walk away.

❧

Joe had installed the cappuccino machine that morning and asked the only civilian employee on his payroll to organize the coffee station with the new supplies. Pam had worked the day desk since before he'd been there and knew as much about daily operations as he did.

The first shift had enjoyed their cappuccinos and even radioed the deputies in the field to stop by on their breaks. Next thing he knew, they were going to want bistro tables and a lounge area. "Those cups are disposable," he said to anyone who happened by. "That means you take your cappuccino and go."

At nine a.m. he had a call on his cell and closed his office door.

"Photos are in your email. I overnighted fingerprints and DNA. You should be getting that today," the PI said.

Joe immediately opened his email software. The photos of Laurel and her silver-haired companion were surprisingly clear and several showed her and her companion close-up. He focused on the unfamiliar man's face, noting he was definitely old enough to be her father. He was clean-shaven, dressed in inconspicuous gray trousers and a subtle blue shirt, wearing a watch and a wedding ring. On closer inspection, the man had nearly invisible hearing aids.

There was no fear or concern on Laurel's face. Was that what he'd been hoping for?

"Did they exchange anything?" Joe asked.

"Nothing. They talked for almost two hours. The female seemed animated at times, and he smiled at her often. He paid for the meal and walked her to her car in the parking garage, where he hugged her. I followed the guy to his hotel."

Joe jotted down the hotel and room number. "Did you see anything that seemed off? Anything suspicious? How did she react to this guy?"

"When she arrived, she checked out the entire place," the PI answered. "Like making sure she wasn't being followed. Like a person who's hiding from someone or something. That was my observation. She didn't notice me. The two of them didn't seem like family. My impression was business or acquaintances, probably because the hug was a little awkward."

"Okay, this is good info. Email me an invoice," Joe told him. "Thanks."

He gave the head of security at the lodge a call and offered to buy him coffee and pie at Pearl's.

He studied the photos, uncomfortable that Laurel had been photographed without her knowledge, but still believing the invasion of privacy was justified. Laurel didn't seem capable of hiding distress, and the photos showed none of her triggers in her demeanor.

He would wait for the evidence to be delivered, but if this guy was someone shady, he didn't want to risk the guy checking out of that hotel and disappearing. Accomplished criminals could be proficient at blending in and appearing nondescript. He grabbed his coat and hat and told Pam he had something to follow up on.

While he trudged toward the cafe, he texted Deke Ward that he was on the way over. Deke's reply told him he was already at a booth.

"Ordered you a cup of coffee," his poker buddy said.

"I just put in a cappuccino machine, so you'll have to forgive me if I pass."

Deke grinned. "I take it the deputies are well caffeinated?"

Joe shook his head. "Bunch of grown men acting like it's a new toy."

"Something on your mind?"

Joe took the rolled-up photos from his pocket and hung his coat on a hook before sitting. He glanced around, making sure they weren't being observed. "I need to find out who this guy is. The female is Laurel Whitaker. She lives in Ben Rumford's rental beside me."

"I know who she is. She was vetted before Jakob offered her a job."

"I figured as much. And I've done my own investigations. I'm suspicious that there's something I don't know, and I can't let it go. She has all the signs of abuse or trauma. Her history before her twenties is untraceable, which is fishy. Claims she has no family. But she met this man in Denver this morning. My guy said she wasn't skittish around him."

Deke studied the photo. "Could she be in WITSEC? He might be a U.S. Marshal."

"I thought of that too. It would explain legally sealed

records and authentic identification with a new name," Joe said. "It would explain her not talking about family and not making friends for a number of years. My man didn't think he behaved like a lawman though. She was the one who checked out the restaurant."

"If she's on the run, there are probably reports some-where," Deke said. "Restraining orders, domestic abuse accounts, something."

"Nothing shows up with her name or description, but I don't even have an exact location. DNA samples should arrive today," Joe told him. "Think we can submit those and run face recognition?"

"Your instincts are always good," Deke told him. "I'll run everything past my connections."

"Thing is I don't want this guy to take off before we get something on him." With his elbows on the table, Joe steepled his fingers against his chin as he thought.

"Want someone to go talk to him?"

"I want to do it myself. Today."

"Want me to go with you?"

"No. I've got it."

Deke shrugged. "Keep me informed of every step. I need to be able to send backup if there's trouble."

Joe stood. He trusted his friend. Deke had wisdom and experience. "The drive is two and a half hours each way, so I need to make a plan for my kid in case I'm late getting back, and then I'm taking off." He laid cash on the table. "Order yourself a piece of pie."

Laurel probably wasn't even back yet.

Thankfully, the weather was cold, but no precipitation was forecasted. He changed clothes and took the depart-ment's unmarked 2010 Explorer because it was inconspicu-ous, and he drove Highway 36 southeast skirting Estes and Boulder to reach Denver at rush hour. He grabbed a sandwich across the street and watched the front of the hotel from inside the café.

To his surprise, he recognized the man from the photo enter the café and order takeout. Joe's instincts went on high alert as he observed the person. The man paid and took his purchase. Joe followed, tossing his trash as he headed for the exit. He caught up to the man as he reached the opposite curb.

"I need to talk to you," he said.

The man stopped and turned to face him. "Who are you?"

"You met with a young woman at Brookside Café this morning."

The silver-haired man turned back. "I don't know what you're talking about."

"I have photos, so don't deny it."

The man faced Joe. A muscle ticked in his jaw. "How much do you want?"

"For what?"

"The pictures. How much do you want for the pictures?"

The question stumped Joe. He gathered his thoughts. "I'm not selling them."

"Blackmail then? You've got nothing on me."

"What are you talking about?"

"This isn't my first rodeo, mister. Either name your price or take a hike."

"You misunderstood. All I want is information."

"I'm not selling information." He entered the revolving doors, leaving Joe on the street.

Tamping down confusion, he followed right behind him, entering the hotel lobby on his prey's heels. "I know you met with the person known as Laurel Whitaker this morning. I think she's in trouble, and I'm not laying off until I know your involvement." He took his badge from inside his coat and let the guy have a long look. "Sheriff Cavanaugh. Rockwell County."

The man's expression showed surprise and then resignation. "You're not a reporter?"

"I'm a law officer. And a friend of Laurel's."

"So, you're Joe."

That caught Joe completely off guard. He nodded.

"Come on upstairs."

Joe waited with him for the elevator and let the man lead the way to his room on the fifth floor. He waved his card in front of the sensor and opened the door.

The room was neat, the bed made, an open suitcase on the luggage rack.

"Is your name Jim?" he asked.

The man nodded and set his supper on the desk.

"Are you a U.S. Marshal?"

"What? No." He shook his head. "I was a civil engineer for thirty-five years. Now I'm retired and I like to fish. I'm heading for Rocky Mountain National Park tomorrow."

"Which lake?" Joe asked.

"Pettingell and then Poudre."

Seemed legit. "How do you know Laurel?"

"I don't know that that's any of your business." He seated himself on the desk chair and pointed for Joe to take a seat.

Joe perched on a chair. "I know something is wrong. Laurel has all the signs of a runaway or maybe an abuse survivor or someone in the Witness Protection Program. If she's in trouble, I need to know about it. If someone is looking for her, if she's in any kind of danger—."

"She's not. Not danger like you're thinking. You're going to have to take my word for it."

"But she is hiding," he tested.

"If she wanted you to know, she would tell you."

He couldn't accept that without information. Without facts. This fellow seemed like a nice guy. He also knew something Joe wanted to learn. "I'm not going to give up," he said.

"Your DNA is on my desk right now. I'm sending it out for matches tomorrow. Is anything going to show up?"

Jim's lips flattened and he took a breath. He appeared decidedly uncomfortable.

"Will your DNA show me something you don't want me to know?"

The man looked him in the eye then, and Joe had the distinct impression he felt like an animal caught in a trap. He was out of options, and escaping was impossible. He got up and went to a black case on the floor.

Joe tensed. His revolver was in a holster under his jacket. He made sure his jacket was unzipped and then rested his hand on his thigh.

Jim took out a laptop and carried it to the desk.

Joe relaxed.

After opening it, he turned it on, found his browser and typed in his name: James Denning. The name didn't ring a bell.

Several searches came up on Google, and Jim tapped the second one on the list. A news report pulled up.

James Denning, one of several suspects in the murder of Charlene Greene and the kidnapping of ten-year-old Meryl Greene, was investigated and released Tuesday. Denning discovered the girl in a hunting cabin, where she'd been abandoned. The child was suffering from cuts and bruises, hunger and dehydration. She reportedly had erratic blood pressure and showed signs of post-traumatic stress upon admission to St. Mary's Hospital.

"I was fingerprinted for this investigation," he said. "This is what you'll find."

"I don't understand," Joe said, attempting to clear a cloud of confusion from his head. He looked again at the headlines, the date and location. "Seventeen years ago. I recognize the child's name."

Jim met his eyes with a nod. "Everyone does."

His heart felt like it was sinking to his stomach. He reached for the laptop, turned the screen toward him and clicked on some of the other search results. Photos, front page headlines, a murder case, a kidnapped child.

He looked at the pictures of a dark-haired, dark-eyed, pale and scrawny little girl, a couple of elementary school pictures, a black and white hospital photo showing a pathetically thin child with facial lacerations, and several candid shots obviously taken by newspaper photographers.

"This is Laurel," he admitted to himself, scanning the details. "Her mother was murdered, and she was kidnapped and abandoned."

"The guy was one of her mother's strung-out boyfriends. They fought and he hit her with something and killed her. Meryl saw the whole thing."

"Her name was Meryl."

"When Monte Swan realized what he'd done and that Meryl had seen it, he grabbed her up and stuffed her into the trunk of his car."

Joe ran a hand over his face. "Oh my God."

"Sometime later, he careened off the road, overturning the car, and was apparently knocked unconscious. The next day, he woke up, probably remembering little of the previous night. He opened the trunk and dragged her into the woods to hide. He found a hunting shack. No one knows what he intended to do with her, but eventually his own hunger and need for drugs drove him to abandon her bound and gagged."

"And these articles say you found her? How long was she there?"

"It was six days from Charlotte's murder until I found Meryl. She was in bad shape. Terrified and close to death."

"You saved her life."

He nodded with tears in his eyes. "That day—that moment I found her—it's always in my head."

Joe's throat was so thick with emotion, he could barely speak. He looked at the man. This truth was the last thing he'd expected. "They caught the guy and found him guilty. I remember reading about the case and the trial."

Jim nodded. "After she'd recovered, Laurel was released into the custody of the state to be raised in foster care. Swan's trial was plastered across the media for months, so everyone knew who she was."

"Found guilty and sentenced to life," Joe added.

"He died in prison about six years ago. Getting stabbed by another inmate was too easy of a death for him." He closed the laptop. "Meryl was hounded by reporters and photographers throughout her school years. It was tough getting foster care parents who would deal with it. Several child victim funds aided her education, however. She detested life under the microscopic eyes of classmates and the relentless reporters."

Joe couldn't even wrap his mind around it. "So, she had a private education?"

"As much as possible," Jim replied. "Eventually, she had her court records sealed and her name legally changed."

Joe's heart sank. He'd dug open a deep wound. "And I forced you to betray her confidence."

He looked at Joe. "Your heart is in the right place."

Joe wasn't pleased with himself. He felt sick. Sick about what he'd learned. Sick about what the child Meryl had endured. Sick about what he'd done to find out. Sick that he knew her secret, and she hadn't wanted him to know.

He'd believed she was in danger. "I'm sorry. I forced you to betray her."

"What are you going to do with this information?"

"I won't tell anyone," he said. "You have my word."

"Thank you."

"Do you think…? Could we keep in touch, you and I?"

Jim reached behind the lamp for the pad of hotel paper and a pen and wrote his name and phone number. "If she ever needs me, I'm always available."

Joe stood and extended a hand. Jim got to his feet and put both hands around Joe's. "I have a feeling you'll take care of her."

"If she'll let me. She's pretty good at taking care of herself."

"That's a lifetime of self-defense," he replied.

Joe left the hotel and walked to his car. He stopped in a shop and bought caramel popcorn and fudge to take to Chloe, as well as almond bark for his mom. He located the Explorer in the parking garage, got in and turned on the engine to let it warm.

The enormity of what he'd done combined with the enormity of what he'd learned caught up to him. He had a daughter of his own. He remembered Chloe at ten, skinny legs and curly ponytail, a kid with no mom. But she'd always had him, always had a big extended family. She'd never gone hungry or been terrified of anything more frightening than a silly circus clown. He'd kept the truth about her mother from her so she didn't have to deal with that along with having a mom who'd left. If anything like this had happened to her, he'd have wanted to kill the person himself.

He couldn't wipe the dark-eyed child in those photographs from his head. No wonder Laurel had social issues; no wonder she had mild claustrophobia. Her life in the public eye must have been her own private nightmare.

She might be the bravest person he knew.

His eyes stung. His nose burned.

Sitting in the darkened garage in the enclosed vehicle, Joe wept. He covered his mouth with a fist, and his shoulders shook. He wept for the innocent child who'd had no one to love or comfort her. He wept for the young woman who'd put on a brave face and reinvented herself to survive in this harsh world.

Once he'd exhausted the rush of emotion, he found paper napkins and wiped his face. He called Deke to let him know to call off all investigations because this wasn't at all what he'd imagined. "I'm heading home."

What was he going to do now?

CHAPTER TWELVE

One of Laurel's secret desires in recreating herself into a strong capable woman was to let go and have a little fun—do something impulsive—wear something bright and not care if she drew attention.

She'd ordered the perfect off-the-shoulder vintage-style dress for Christmas, and it still hung in her closet with its tags. She pulled it out and stepped into it for the first time. She'd thought she might have to send it back, but the side zipper made getting into it easy, and the garment fit perfectly. The fitted red bodice bared her shoulders. A red and green plaid fabric had been sewn to the bottom of the solid red skirt in a diagonal hemline, so the plaid pattern draped across the front from her left hip to her right ankle. It was definitely unique and bold. And fun. She chose black heels with ankle straps and put her identification and lipstick in a sequined black clutch. Red lipstick complimented her ensemble.

Laurel smiled at herself in the mirror. "You're going to a party." She checked her sparkly black earrings. "You have a date."

Her stomach dipped. She felt like a teenager.

This was definitely a date. He'd invited her to a dinner party in advance. It was not a family gathering, and his daughter would not be joining them. It didn't get any more adult than this.

She'd already met several residents who would be there, and Joe was one of the most respected people in Spencer. No one was going to put her on the spot, and she would fit in. She had nothing to fear.

A loud rap on the front door startled her, and she hurried to let in Joe.

"You look beautiful," he said, and his appreciative expression backed up his words.

"Thank you. You look handsome yourself." He wore a full-length coat over what looked to be dress slacks and shiny black shoes.

She carried her coat from the closet, and he took it from her. She turned away to let him help her, and he pulled the garment up over her shoulders. She'd held up her hair, and he lowered his face to nuzzle her neck. "You smell so good."

His warm breath against her skin created a shiver that spread from her neck, across her shoulders, and down her spine.

"I almost wish I wasn't hosting this party so that I could keep you here all to myself this evening." After she lowered her hair over her collar, he wrapped his arms around her. With a sigh, she laid her head back against his shoulder.

She reached up to place her palm against his freshly-shaven jaw. The warm unfamiliar texture reminded her she was out of her element, but each new experience with this man was exciting. Her mind flitted over his words about staying home alone, and she turned to meet his gaze. "We'd better go."

She flicked off the lights, and he led her to his vehicle.

"What's Chloe doing this evening?" she asked.

"She's staying the night with Avery over at Colette and Tyler's. They have a bed for her."

Located in Olde Town, The Golden Grille was an upscale restaurant with a definite romantic atmosphere. They checked their coats and were directed to a party room, where a few people had already gathered. There were no uniforms in sight.

Joe introduced her to Pam, who he claimed ran the office, and her husband. A server immediately took their drink order and brought them a bottle of wine and glasses.

"Laurel, this is Frank Davies," Joe said, gesturing to a stout middle-aged fellow. "Elaine," he said to the man's wife, "This Is Laurel Whitaker."

"Hello, dear," she greeted Laurel with a warm smile. "I had no idea the sheriff had found himself such a lovely friend. That dress is stunning. If I had to guess, I'd say you're one of the celebrities we pretend not to notice."

Laurel's cheeks warmed. "Not at all. You're too kind. I'm a plain old social media manager, marketer and website designer. I'm usually at home, dressed in jeans."

Jericho spotted them and led a pretty young woman over. Holding a foamy glass of beer, he said with a grin, "This is my hot date."

Joe leaned forward and gave the girl a peck on the cheek. She turned and punched Jericho in the arm, then said to Laurel, "I'm his sister, Bethel. You must be the gorgeous new lodge employee I've heard about."

Laurel was still uncomfortable with compliments. "Well, I'm contracted with the lodge anyway."

"I run Little Grizzlies, the childcare at the lodge," Bethel said.

"I saw that on the website," Laurel told her. "It looks amazing in the photos."

"We try to make it fun as well as educational, because we have about twenty regulars who are kids of staff members.

So, it's pretty much like preschool and summer camp rolled into one."

"I'd love to come see the facility," Laurel said.

"As long as you have lodge security clearance, I can give you a tour. I heard it was your idea to add pet daycare. That's brilliant."

"I did suggest it." She sipped her wine to cover her self-consciousness.

Vida Lucas, the other self-defense instructor joined them. Laurel had never seen her in anything other than yoga pants and a tank top. The other woman's slim black dress showed off her fit shape and toned arms.

"There's no way you could conceal a weapon in that dress," Bethel told her. "Good thing you know how to defend yourself, because you look *hot*."

Vida laughed and waved away the teasing compliment. "The county only treats us once a year, and I'm taking full advantage of free dinner and wine." She checked out Joe's stunning appearance in his shirt and tie. "Hello, Sheriff. You clean up real nice."

"You're not so bad yourself."

Laurel enjoyed their light-hearted conversations. This was probably a much-needed break from their responsibilities and often serious discussions and dangerous jobs. When they seated themselves at the long banquet-style table, Joe held out her chair, then slid his close beside her. His deep brown gaze glided over her face and hair, pausing to appreciate her bare shoulders. A flicker of unease passed over his features, but then he smiled, found her fingers, and rested their clasped hands in her lap.

She remembered the first time she'd seen him in the basement of the newspaper morgue, how huge and intimidating he'd seemed. Her heart still thumped in her chest when she looked at him, but now for a completely different and foreign reason. But this reason felt good.

The table was set with small loaves of bread, plates of butter pats and salad dressings. An efficient staff of six men and women in black trousers and white shirts served their dinner salads and took more drink orders. The main course came next. An enormous fragrant steak filled Joe's plate, a loaded baked potato on the side, and the sever placed a seafood platter in front of her.

She glanced around, noting most of the deputies had ordered steaks, but here and there was a salmon dinner or crisp trout.

"I'm never going to be able to eat all this," she said quietly, while looking at the crab legs, tender-looking lobster and huge shrimp all nestled in a bed of grilled zucchini slices, quartered ears of corn, and lemon halves.

"You can take home what you don't eat," he assured her. He pointed to her plate. "May I?"

She was surprised, but answered, "Yes, of course."

He took a piece of corn and a jumbo shrimp. "Want a bite of my steak?"

Was this what couples did when they went out together? She nodded. "Yes, I'd like to try it."

He sliced her off a portion and set it on her bread plate.

Laurel enjoyed the delicious flavors, the conversation around them, but most especially the experience. This was what normal people did. She'd first participated in a family Thanksgiving, and now she'd eaten with work friends. This was Joe's life. Easy, companionable, comforting. A sensory overload she welcomed and savored.

Previously, she'd noted how much the man could consume, so it was no surprise he finished his steak and ate a couple of her crab legs. While the servers cleared the table, she excused herself to use the restroom and wash her hands. Joe accompanied her to the small hallway. When she came out of the restroom, he was leaning against the wall, waiting for her. He gently wrapped his fingers around her bare arm and drew her up against him.

Voices and sounds of dishes and glassware came from the kitchen area nearby. She looked up and their eyes met. Neither said anything, but both leaned into the other until their lips met. He tilted his head and kissed her long and deep.

Finally, he moved back and took her hand. "Shall we?"

Shall we what? she wondered, and then corralled her thoughts. They took their seats, and she glanced at him, noting the trace of red lipstick on his lower lip. She handed him her napkin and indicated he should wipe his mouth. He did and looked at the smear on the white napkin.

She lowered her head to hide her grin.

When she looked across the table, Bethel Tanner wore an amused smile. "I wonder what's for dessert."

The servers showed up a few minutes later with trays and set desserts in front of each person. Slices of four-layer chocolate cake displayed on a caramel drizzled plate and garnished with raspberries. From around the table, the guests voiced murmurs of appreciation.

Picking up her dessert fork, Laurel glanced up at Joe. "You really know how to throw a dinner party."

He acknowledged her remark with a tilt of his head and refilled her wine glass.

Dessert was a delectable memory by the time the deputies and their plus ones filtered from the party room and made their way outside into the now-frigid mountain air.

Laurel and Joe huddled together in his truck while the engine warmed the interior, and then he drove eastward toward midtown.

"Mom's decorating her tree tomorrow afternoon. Will you come with Chloe and I? It's only family."

"Your 'only family' is a crowd."

"I guess so. But it's casual. We eat popcorn and drink hot

chocolate. Brooke usually cooks up a big pot of soup. No pressure. Only if you want to."

"I want to." She surprised herself. She'd seen how the Cavanaughs did Thanksgiving, and she wanted to know how their family celebrated Christmas. She looked over. "I do."

He took her gloved hand. "Great." A minute later, he pulled from Second Street behind a corner building. "Parking gets tight when we're all here, so I'm going to park right here in this no parking zone behind the vet's office."

"I don't suppose anyone will give the sheriff a ticket," she mused.

"Nope. Sit right there." He got out and came around the truck to her door. "The ground is a little slick, so let me hold onto you in those shoes."

He held open the Wild Card's rear door and ushered her inside, along the hall past the restrooms and the band platform until they reached the bar area, where Joe was greeted by a dozen or more people. Several tables had been reserved, and a deputy waved them over.

"This is Paul Ireland," Joe said.

"We didn't get a chance to meet at dinner," Paul said.

A tall brunette in jeans and a T-shirt came to take their orders. "Hey, Joe. What are you having?"

"Ruby, this is Laurel. Laurel, this is Ruby Leigh. She's also recently relocated to Spencer."

"Hi, Laurel," Ruby said with a smile. "Is this your first visit to the Wild Card?"

Laurel nodded. "Are the margaritas good?"

"The best. Top shelf only. Shaken or blended?"

"Blended, please."

"Atta girl." She winked. "The guys are cooking up a Christmas party here on the twenty-first. Have the two of you heard about it?"

"I think someone mentioned it," Joe answered.

"Be sure to stop by," she said. "Be right back with your drinks."

Joe leaned close. "I have it on good authority that the Christmas party is a cover for a proposal."

"Really? Whose?"

"Hunter Lawe is going to ask Ruby to marry him."

"And she has no idea?"

He shook his head. "It's a surprise."

"What if she says no?"

Joe studied her. "They've been through a lot. If you could see them together, you'd know there's no way she'll say no. She's crazy about him."

"He must be confident that's true," she said.

The band that had been on break returned to the platform and picked up their instruments. The piece began with a drum beat. "*I got my mind set on you,*" the male singer repeated.

"I know this song," he said. "What is it?"

"It's a George Harrison song," she answered.

"*But it's gonna take money, a whole lot of spending money. It's gonna take plenty of money...to do it right, child.*"

"Oh sure." He reached for her hand. "Want to dance?"

She resisted, finishing her delicious margarita as Ruby brought another. "I haven't danced in front of anyone since one of my foster moms made me go to class with her daughter."

"Come on. No one cares. I'm not good either."

She had yet to see anything he wasn't good at, but she let him persuade her from her seat to the dancefloor. Other couples crowded around them, laughing, enjoying themselves, and their enthusiasm and lack of inhibitions were contagious. She moved her feet and legs, and inspired by the elevating music, her body followed.

Joe smiled and spun her around. They danced until the song ended and another started. This one was slower, and he showed her how to two-step by holding both her hands and saying "Quick-quick, slow-slow," until they were in rhythm. Then he took her right hand in his left and put her left hand on his upper arm. He spread his other hand wide over her back. "I lead, and your job is to keep the distance between us, so I don't step on your feet."

"Okay."

"'An' we got yuppies, we got bikers, an' we got thirsty hitchhikers. And the girls next door dress up like movie stars.'" Everyone sang together, *"'Mm, mm, mm, mm, mm, I love this bar.'"*

"You said you weren't good," she said close to his ear.

"Well, I know the etiquette and how not to get run over," he told her. "Faster dancers on the outside of the floor, going counter-clockwise."

They were in the center, which made her laugh.

Around them, a chant had begun, catching her full attention. "Jericho. Jericho. Jericho." She looked at Joe for explanation.

"You'll see," he said.

Joe's deputy left his partner on the dancefloor and made his way to the platform, where he picked up an acoustic guitar and stepped to the microphone. "What do you cowboys and cowgirls want to hear?"

A variety of shouts came from the crowd.

He shook his head and waved them off. "I'm gonna ask my boss. What do you want to hear, Sheriff?"

"Making Memories of Us," Joe called.

"See there? The sheriff knows sexy music," he said into the microphone, and the crowd laughed.

Jericho played the opening chords, and the band joined in with a soft brush on the drum. It was a Keith Urban song that Laurel had loved since the first time she'd heard it. *"'I'm gonna be here for you baby. I'll be a man of my word, speak the language in a voice that you have never heard.'"*

Joe pulled her close and the moment felt so right, so

perfect. She could feel his heartbeat and his warmth. He was strong, comforting. She recalled his breath on her neck before they'd ever left the house. Her reactions to this man were disturbing and pleasurable.

"'And I'm gonna love you like nobody loves you. And I'll earn your trust, making memories of us.'"

She wanted this moment to last forever. She wanted to be the person Joe made her feel as though she could be. She was focusing on the present in a big way.

A commotion with raised voices and the sound of broken glass broke out near the bar. Heads turned to see what was happening. Joe looked up at Jericho and signaled that the band should keep playing. "I'll be right back," he said to Laurel and left her standing on the dancefloor.

Most of the couples stopped dancing, and Laurel had a clear view of Joe's broad back in his white shirt as he approached the two men scuffling.

"Not real bright to pick a fight in a bar full of deputies," Vida said from close beside her. "Don't worry. Joe and Frank have this."

Laurel recognized the man Joe restrained as one of the men who'd helped work on the interior of Joe's home. "That's the outfitter."

"Matt Chandler," Vida verified. "He's been a little off the rails since his wife died a few years ago. Doesn't look like it's getting better."

"I met his sister," Laurel said. "She's here visiting him and his children for Christmas."

"Merry friggin' Christmas to them," the deputy replied.

Joe glanced their way and nodded to Vida, then jerked a thumb over his shoulder.

"He's taking Matt over to sleep it off in a cell," she said. "Come on, we'll order fresh drinks."

Twenty minutes later, Joe approached their table and

Vida moved over so he could sit beside Laurel. "He's okay for tonight."

"Charges?" Vida asked.

"Nah. Ace didn't want to make a big deal out of it. No harm was done."

"Who's Ace?" Laurel asked.

"That fella behind the bar now," he replied. "He owns this place." He faced her. "What do you say we head out?"

"Sure. I had a great time, but I'm ready to go."

They stood and said their good-byes. Joe helped her with her coat and again steadied her on the snowy pavement as they walked to his truck. Inside, he turned on the heater, and pulled her close. "I had a good time tonight too. It was almost too enjoyable to have been a work party."

"My dancing wasn't too bad," she said. "Thanks to you."

"I can't wait for you to see Chloe dance," he said.

"I'm looking forward to that."

He leaned over and kissed her. "I'm looking forward to sharing a lot of things with you. Somehow, having you with me, talking to you about things, makes them better."

How he could feel that way about her was a wonder. "I'm not anyone special," she said.

"I disagree." He released her, put the truck in gear and drove toward Twin Owl Lake. When they'd nearly reached her place, he said, "Sorry about the interruption back there."

"You don't have to apologize. You're the sheriff. It comes with the job. Sorry about your friend."

He reached for her gloved hand. "It's a tough situation. His wife took her own life."

"That's awful. He must have a lot of confusing feelings. Does he get counseling?"

"He won't talk about it to me, so I don't know."

"We don't walk in other people's shoes, so we don't know what they're going through."

He entered her drive and parked close to the house. "You're a kind-hearted person, Laurel."

"Come in, Joe," she said.

He held her by the waist as they walked to the door, where she unlocked it and preceded him inside. Tossing his coat over the back of a chair, he helped her out of hers.

Immediately, she leaned into him and framed his face between her hands. "I don't want this evening to end."

He kissed her gently at first, then angling his head and stroking her bare shoulders. "I don't have to be anywhere," he whispered into her ear, sending tingles along her spine. "I'm all yours."

"That's a very tempting offer, Sheriff."

"I aim to please."

Their lips met again, this time more urgently, more demanding. Joe explored the length of her back.

"Where is the zipper hidden on this fancy dress?" he asked.

She laughed and took his hand.

CHAPTER THIRTEEN

*J*oe woke to a delicious warmth along his side. He turned to his side to get his fill of this incredible woman with whom he'd fallen head over heels in love. She lay facing him, a cascade of dark hair draped over one eye and part of her face. Gently, he moved the silky skein over her shoulder so he could gaze his fill.

Her dark brows were perfect slender arches. She had a slim straight nose, full inviting lips and satiny pale skin. She took his breath away. Everything about her made his chest feel tight with emotion. He felt like a teenager with his first crush on the prettiest girl in school.

Her childhood and the trauma she'd endured only made him admire her more. She might look like as fragile as a butterfly's wings, but she was strong and resilient. Strength took a toll, however.

Laurel took a deep breath and her eyes opened, focusing to pierce him with the alluring abyss of her dark gaze. He could easily lose himself in her eyes.

"Good morning," he said.

Her mouth curved into a shy smile, which he quickly covered with a kiss. "Sorry. I need to shave."

She laid her palm along his cheek and caressed his skin with her thumb. "I don't mind. I probably look a mess."

"To the contrary." He ran a finger over her eyebrow. "Looking at you takes my breath away. You are perfection. I love everything about you...your deep, dark eyes and your eyelashes, your skin and the shape of your mouth...the way it changes your whole face when you smile."

Her lips curved into a soft smile.

"But besides all that...you're you."

She seemed to be discerning his words. Taking in the complexity of meaning.

"I've never known anyone like you," he said.

"I've never known anyone like *you*," she replied.

He rested his hand over her cheek and temple. "The fact that you look at me like I'm someone special...well, that's almost more than my heart can handle."

A new sheen glistened in her eyes. "You are someone special," she whispered.

He kissed her tenderly and folded her into his arms. They lay that way for a long time until his phone dinged a message.

He leaned away to reach for his phone. "It's Stephanie. She went to early church with mom, and they'll be fixing a noon meal if we want to get our butts in gear."

Laurel sat and opened her screen to check the time. "We've missed breakfast, so we'd better go for lunch. You might blow away if you don't eat."

He sat on the side of the bed. "No headache this morning?" he asked.

"Maybe a wee bit. I didn't drink that much. You?"

"I'm good. I was just wondering…."

"What?"

"If you had any regrets."

She had started to rise, but she walked on her knees across the bed to come up behind him and wrap her arms around him. "My only regret is that I didn't meet you sooner."

He turned his head against hers and covered her hand on his chest with his. "We have plenty of time."

She kissed his neck. "I'm going to shower. Help yourself to the coffeemaker."

While she showered, he made coffee, found eggs and scrambled a pan full. She'd probably laugh, but he was starving.

When she joined him, dressed and looking fresh and prettier than ever, he gave her a plate of eggs. While she ate, he washed the pan. His gut screamed for him to tell her he was in love with her, to make a commitment, but there was too much left unsaid.

He knew her story. He knew the thing she worked diligently to keep hidden. Maybe last night had been unfair. She didn't know what he'd done.

She wouldn't reveal her secret on her own, he was certain.

In order to live with himself…in order to move forward, he was going to have to tell her.

❦

Chloe met them at the kitchen door and bestowed hugs. He embraced his daughter and kissed the top of her head.

"Avery and I had so much fun last night." She took a step back. "We have to sing you the funny song we made up. We made a video of it. Did you have fun at your work party?"

"We had a good time, yes."

"Did you dance?" She twisted to pointedly look over her shoulder at Laurel.

Laurel gave her a smug smile. "As a matter of fact, we did."

"Take our coats, please, pumpkin," her dad requested, and she bounced away with their wraps.

His mom's home smelled wonderful. Brooke had cooked up two gigantic kettles of chili, one spicey, the other mild. The counter was laden with crackers, an impressive cheese assortment, and a bowl of sour cream with chives.

"How do you have fresh chives in the winter?" Laurel asked.

"I freeze them in bags all during the summer," Liz replied. "I made potato soup for the delicate eaters."

"That would be me," Avery claimed, selecting a bowl from the towering mismatched stack on the island.

Joe and his brothers, as well as Brooke, dug into the spicy chili, while the other women and kids ate the mild version. Tyler and Crosby stopped periodically to blow their noses and wipe their eyes.

"How is that even enjoyable?" Colette asked.

"You drink milk along with it, to balance out the heat," Dusty replied. After two servings, he carried his bowl to the sink, where Kendra was rinsing and loading the dishwasher. He leaned around her to rinse his own bowl and spoon, then loaded them.

Over her shoulder, Kendra gave him a tender smile. Dusty moved a tendril of hair behind her ear, and they shared a private smile.

Joe glanced at Laurel, noting she'd been watching their exchange as well. She glanced at him and gave him a tremulous smile. Joe understood her hesitation and lack of certainty in unfamiliar situations better than he wanted to. She'd been on her own, living a solitary life to avoid people so long that she'd likely never been around two people in love. All his life, he'd had his parents' relationship as an example.

"The soups will be warm whenever anyone wants a refill," Stephanie said as her siblings made their way out of the kitchen.

"Crosby and I picked out the tree yesterday," Liz

explained. "He set it up last night, so it had time to fall out. We need young helpers to carry boxes from the storeroom. They're all sitting out and labeled."

Crosby and the teenagers carried stacks of boxes and plastic totes into the enormous living room. His nephew, Ian, came to perch beside Joe on the window seat. "I don't believe in Santa Claus anymore."

"No?" Joe asked hesitantly. "Who brings all those presents?"

"My dad and Kendra. Last year I saw three different Santas at the mall, and another one came to school. All different. Plus, I'd been wondering about that whole chimney thing for a long time. I figured it out then."

"Were you disappointed?" Joe asked.

"Nah. It's easier to tell my folks what I want than to write a dumb letter."

Grinning, Joe ruffled his fair hair. "I can see that."

The lights went on the tree first, with Stephanie directing Crosby who was on a ladder, and Tyler and Dusty standing on either side of the tree.

"This is a pretty complex strategy," Laurel commented.

"With Stephanie, everything is a strategic undertaking," Joe replied. "She oversees the floral arrangements and holiday displays at the lodge too."

"I think some families sit around and toss tinsel at the tree over hot chocolate," Crosby said loud enough for his sister to overhear.

"Only the families not up for a Cavanaugh Christmas," Steph replied.

"Which is only everyone else," Brooke said from her seat with her legs tucked under her on the sofa. She directed a comment to Laurel. "I get my turn when the sentimental stuff comes out."

After the dozens of light strands met Steph's approval, his mom opened her boxes of garland and lifted out strands.

Beside him, Laurel sucked in a surprised breath. He glanced at her.

"They're all so beautiful," she said.

"I've been collecting them since the first Christmas my husband and I were married," Liz explained. His mom's treasure trove of sparkling glass bead garland went on next, ropes and ropes draping from the branches.

"I remember a town square when I was small," Laurel said. "I can't remember where it was, because I lived a lot of places, but there was an enormous Christmas tree with beads dangling from the branches. I thought it was the most beautiful thing I'd ever seen." She stopped as though embarrassed to have revealed something personal. "Well, since then I've only seen trees like this in Christmas movies."

"I love Christmas movies," Brooke chimed in. "We seriously do need hot chocolate while we trim the tree. And popcorn."

Kyle got up and headed for the kitchen. "I'll make the popcorn."

"I'll help!" Ian ran after him.

"Then we'll have to bake gingerbread cookies," Liz added with a grin.

"But the snow's too dry for a good snowball fight," Colette said with dramatic exaggeration. "And where's the mistletoe?"

"That's comes on Christmas Eve," Kendra explained.

"The heck with mistletoe. I can't wait for the popcorn," Crosby added.

"How can you even think about eating again?" Laurel asked.

Her serious question following their sarcasm had everyone laughing.

Joe turned to scoop her close and hug her.

❧

Brooke took over handling the box of sentimental ornaments, holding each piece aloft while the maker or their mother explained whose small fingers had crafted each wooden clothespin, popsicle stick, cotton ball, pinecone and scrap of construction paper with paint and glitter into a reindeer or angel or Santa. These were Liz's treasures, her memories of Christmases with her children, mementos of days she cherished.

Laurel's throat tightened at the emotional connection these people shared as a family, their precious memories. This home was filled with remembrances of times together, of parents who had secretly shopped and wrapped and left the perfect gifts under the tree only to watch their children's delighted faces on Christmas morning.

Using her sleeve, Laurel dabbed tears from her eyes. She could watch these people and listen to their stories and memories all day. This was better than any movie.

Joe noticed and wrapped his arm around her shoulders. "Are you all right?"

"I'm great." She smiled up at him. "Really."

By late afternoon, the tree was decorated, lights twinkling, the branches loaded with an abundance of old and new ornaments. Laurel had changed her thinking about that tree in the town square so long ago. *This* was the most beautiful tree she'd ever seen, better than anything from a magazine or a movie, because everything on it had significance.

"Dad, can I go with Aunt Colette and Uncle Tyler to pick out their tree?" Chloe asked.

"Did they invite you?"

She nodded. "Uncle Tyler did. He invited Ian along too. He said they'd drop me off at home later. Please?"

"Give me a hug before you go."

She squeezed him around the waist. "You're the best."

"Don't forget it."

She bounded off to join her cousins.

Laurel helped Liz and Stephanie pour leftover chili into quart jars, clean the stove and wipe the counters.

"Take a jar home, Laurel," Liz said.

"Thank you." She selected potato soup. "You'll have to tell me how you make this."

"I bake the potatoes. Gives it that rich flavor."

They said goodbyes and Laurel accompanied Joe to his truck, which he'd already warmed up. "I admit I was thankful Chloe was going with Tyler," Joe said as he drove. "There's something I want to talk to you about. It's serious."

Her stomach fluttered with nerves. Serious? How serious could it be? Last night and this morning he'd said a lot of things she hadn't had time to process. He thought she was beautiful. She'd always been the pale, skinny girl no one wanted, but he thought she was beautiful. He made her feel valuable, and she loved that about him.

He'd never known anyone like her. She made *him* feel special. Caring made her vulnerable, which was new and frightening. If he intended to weave this fragile thread of their new beginning to something more serious, she was unprepared. What would she say? What if he said he loved her?

The interior of the cab was uncomfortably warm. She peeled away her neck scarf. "I don't know if I'm ready to talk about anything serious."

"We have to talk about this."

He was scaring her now. "Okay."

He pulled into her drive and parked, leaving the engine running.

"What is it?" she asked.

He scrubbed his hand down over his face and pursed his lips. "There's nothing to do, but to say it."

Waiting was wearing on her nerves. "Say it."

"I was concerned about you. About your safety. You're closed off and you keep everything to yourself. I put all the things I knew about you together and suspected you were running from someone. I took your issues into consideration and came to a conclusion."

Her heart tripped uncomfortably.

"I thought you were perhaps running from an abusive boyfriend or husband."

"I told you early on that I'd never been in a serious relationship."

"I know you did. But you weren't sure of me back then, and I suspected you were hiding things to protect yourself. There were a lot of factors that added up. Your extreme need for privacy, your anxiety, going to counseling and taking self-defense classes."

Her anxiety level rose until her cheeks flamed. "Do you think all of your students are taking classes because they're afraid of someone in particular?"

"No."

"Then why me?"

"The facts added up and made sense. It still makes sense that a similar situation might have been the truth."

Her heart threatened to stop. "What did you do?"

"I investigated you."

Her pulse pounded in her ears for a full thirty seconds. "Investigated me how?"

"I have a number of data bases at my disposal and connections across the country."

There was no way he'd discovered her in a data base. "You didn't find anything in those, did you?"

"No."

"Did that make you feel better?"

"No, it frustrated me."

She studied his face, hating the disappointment she was feeling. "You didn't trust me."

"I didn't trust that you were safe, Laurel."

"Did hoping to dig up my past make you feel better?"

"No."

She was angry now, feeling betrayed and vulnerable. "I can't believe you investigated me. I thought we were building a relationship."

"Were we?"

She only looked at him, as uncertain now of this person beside her as she'd been the first time she'd seen him.

He gestured with his open hand. "You never told me anything. What was I supposed to think?"

That hurt. Her chest ached. "I had my reasons, Joe."

"I know that now."

Silence lapsed between them.

His words swirled in her consciousness and settled like a rock of reality in her gut. "What does that mean?"

He took a shaky breath. "I saw the note on your calendar. You were planning to meet someone in Denver. I had you followed."

Additional heat flashed up her body to her neck and face, and she trembled. She attempted to raise a hand to her head, but it shook, and she dropped it to her lap. "You had me followed? Like a criminal?"

"I was scared for you."

"And then what?"

"And then I found out who the person was and confronted him."

She buried her face in her hands. "Oh, no. Oh, no, you didn't. Tell me you didn't go talk to him."

"I talked to him."

"He wouldn't have told you anything."

"He had to. I had his DNA, and he knew that would lead me to the records and the articles about being a suspect in your mother's death."

All the air sucked from the cab of the truck. She couldn't breathe. Laurel unlocked her door and pushed it open with force, jumping out to the gravel drive. Like a drowning person coming to the surface, she gulped in the cold air. "You had no right to do that. You had no right to go behind my back and dig up something that was none of your business."

"I know," he said. "I'm sorry. I thought I was protecting you."

"By exposing me? By digging up everything I've spent my whole life burying? You betrayed me, Joe. You didn't respect me enough to accept my wishes and have a relationship on my terms."

"You're right. I'm sorry."

She slammed the door and trudged toward the house. The driver door slammed behind her. "Don't follow me!"

"Let me explain. I thought you were in danger. I wanted to help."

With shaking hands, she unlocked her front door. "I didn't want your help. I wanted your respect. I wanted you to see me as the person I am now, not the victim I was then."

"Laurel—"

Facing the wood panel in front of her, she held up a hand. "Don't look at me. I don't want your pity. I'm not pathetic."

"I don't pity you. I'm sad for you, but I don't pity you. You're the bravest person I know. Braver than me."

"Go get my soup."

"What?"

"My soup. It's in the truck."

He strode back, returned with her jar of soup, and handed it to her. "Can I come in? We can talk this through."

"I know what I need to know. You know what you obviously need to know." Finally, she turned to look him in the eyes. "Are you going to tell anyone?"

"No. Of course not. I won't say anything to anyone."

"I don't know if I trust you. I don't know if I might need to leave."

As though she'd inflicted a wound, he spread a hand over his chest where his coat hung open. "You have my word,

Laurel. No matter what happens, I'll never breathe a word to a soul. Please don't leave. Don't disappear. Let me show you I can be trusted."

She stepped inside before his rugged tenderness could make her question her sensibilities again. "Don't come back. Don't call me."

She closed the door in his face.

A minute later his truck turned around and drove toward the road.

There. That proved it. She had lived years with the prevailing fear that something bad was going to happen, something elusive, something that would rip her paper-thin life out from under her. It had happened. And Joe Cavanaugh had delivered the blow.

CHAPTER FOURTEEN

*L*aurel felt as though she was ten years old again. Abandoned, left for dead, trapped in a dark place, bound so she couldn't move. No one would come for her. No one cared. All the progress she'd made, years of therapy, all those painful steps only to end up here with an ache so deep and yawning, she couldn't take a breath without suffocating pain.

After standing under the hot water in the shower until it ran cold, she dried herself and her hair and put on pajamas. Her first inclination was to strip the bed and put on clean sheets, so she did, but then when she curled up around her pillow, she cried. Getting up, she retrieved the sheets from the hamper, wadded them up and held them to her chest.

Alone again. Always alone. How was this fair? She hated herself for her self-pity.

This wasn't how her new beginning was supposed to have gone.

Why had Joe pushed so hard, dug so deep? Why couldn't he have accepted her and left well enough alone?

She tried to watch television. Images and snips of their conversation replayed over and over in her head. She couldn't concentrate on a program, but the background noise was better than silence. It took hours to fall asleep.

Laurel dreamed she was with Joe in the same old-fashioned delivery van she'd dreamed of before. He drove along rutted roads until they were lost. Her phone wouldn't work, so she couldn't use GPS or call for help. A small house with a broken trellis beside the porch came into view. She recognized it as the last place she'd lived with her mother. "I don't want to stop here," she told him.

Joe parked and got out of the truck.

"Don't go in there!" she shouted.

He ignored her warning. "Barney is there."

A mangy yellow lab emerged from the side of the house, growled at Joe, its hackles up, teeth bared. The canine's fur was matted with blood.

"Joe, let's go!" she called to him. "Get in the truck."

Joe walked closer to the animal.

Fear rose in Laurel's chest, and she could barely breathe around it. Something terrible was going to happen. She couldn't sit here like a coward and let him be mauled.

"Chloe is in the house," Joe said. "I have to get to her."

She got out of the vehicle. Barney still growled menacingly. "I'll help you find her." She walked closer to the dog and held up a hand. "Barney. Sit. Now."

The dog sat and wagged its tail.

"That's a good boy."

He gave a woof and turned toward the house, as though they should follow.

This was only Barney, and he was leading them to Chloe. "It's okay," she told Joe. "He's helping us."

Weeds grew between the cracks in the crumbling sidewalk, and the porch stairs sagged. A doll with a broken face lay beside the screen door. Joe stood right behind her. A fly batted against the screen. From inside the house came faint music—something oddly familiar, but she couldn't place the song.

Joe reached around her, grabbed the latch, and opened the door with a squeak.

A woman's feet were visible on the floor around the end of a lumpy sofa. Laurel recognized the worn soles on those silver house slippers. Her heart leapt in her chest. This person wasn't Chloe, and she couldn't bear facing the scene lying in wait.

She turned and ran smack into an immovable broad chest.

Hands clamped around her upper arms.

But the man wasn't Joe.

She couldn't scream, couldn't run, couldn't save herself or Chloe, wherever she was.

Laurel jerked awake and sat up in bed, her heart pounding, her pajama top damp with perspiration. None of it had been real. She fought to clear the fogginess of the dream from her head.

Reality wrapped her in its own nightmare as she remembered the events of the evening.

Joe.

She yearned for the security of his embrace, his warmth and safety. She'd dared to allow herself a taste of those things, and having known them, she was bereft.

She felt betrayed, alone, angry.

Angry because he hadn't trusted her to handle her own life.

She didn't know where to go from here.

❦

Laurel sat in Dr. Easton's office with a cup of salted caramel coffee. The aroma wasn't as comforting today as she remembered.

"Before this development, you'd reached step five," the doctor said. "How did that feel?"

"Deceptively good," she replied. At Dr. Easton's raised brow, she went on. "I was focusing on the present and enjoying it, but maybe I was protecting myself from what was coming next."

"And what came next?"

"It should have been sharing my fears and feelings. But I hadn't worked up to that. Then as I said, Joe investigated me, spoke to Jim, and found out the truth."

"And that felt like a betrayal?"

"Absolutely. I should have been able to tell him when I was ready."

"Do you think you'd ever have been ready?" her therapist asked.

Laurel set down her paper coffee cup and placed both hands on the arms of her chair while she thought. Being dishonest with herself wasn't helpful. "I don't know. Maybe not."

"Have your feelings for Joe changed?"

"My version of myself has changed. I don't want to be the person he sees now."

"Who do you think he sees?"

"A victim."

"Does he really?"

Laurel tucked her hair behind her ear and took an impatient breath. "I would."

"Then you're projecting your own feelings about yourself onto him. He may have suspected you were a victim, but now he knows the truth, and what that reveals is that you're an independent woman capable of caring for yourself." She moved from behind her desk to sit on an upholstered chair across from Laurel. "What has actually changed because Joe knows about your childhood?"

Laurel only shook her head.

"You have been defining yourself since before you came to Spencer. You've been defining yourself throughout all of our sessions, with the steps you've taken, with the person you decided to be. You've become more confident, more comfortable with yourself. You've seen yourself as powerful enough to land a career-changing job. Every step of this journey, you have shown up for yourself. That's the person I see. That's the person others see. From what you've told me about the sheriff, I don't believe he thinks less of you or sees you as a victim. He told you you're brave because you are."

Laurel nodded hopefully.

"You have a right to be angry," Dr. Easton pointed out. "But don't give that anger a position above the other things you're feeling. Most of us are more likely to forgive others before we forgive ourselves. Is it possible you're also angry with yourself for not telling him before he found out on his own?"

"You mean he didn't trust me to take care of myself, but I didn't trust him with the truth?" Laurel asked. "Possibly."

"What is step six?" her doctor asked gently.

Laurel took a deep breath. "Express emotions and fear out loud."

"This week think about what you're feeling and what you're afraid of. I believe you'll find some perspective." The therapist went back to her desk and carefully wrote out a note.

Laurel accepted it and read aloud, "'My contentment is not dependent upon external forces or events, but upon me.'"

She smiled at Dr. Easton. "Thank you."

"You're the one who's done all the work. Thank yourself."

Laurel got up and gave her doctor an uncharacteristic hug. The gesture felt right.

She'd left the medical building and was sitting in her car in the parking lot when her phone rang. She didn't recognize the number, but she answered anyway. It might be business.

"Hi, Laurel. Whitney Chandler here. Hope I didn't catch you at a bad time."

"No, it's fine," she said.

"I'm calling because I'm feeling uncomfortable going solo to the Christmas party at the Wild Card tomorrow night. Do you have a date?"

"No, I—"

"That's great. We can go together then. I'm staying at my brother's place out west, and if you're on Twin Owl, you're the opposite direction, so why don't we meet there? In the evening, there's parking at the courthouse or behind the boutiques. How about we meet at the corner of the park across from the Wild Card and walk in together?"

This may not be perfect timing, but she couldn't stay home rehearsing regrets every night. Saying yes had to work out well eventually. "All right. I'll meet you there."

"Perfect. See you then."

❧

Joe spent the day making wellness calls. About once a month the job fell to him, and he didn't mind. First today he'd visited Gladys Kincaid who lived alone in an old house northwest of Spencer. He heard all about her niece, Samantha, serving in Afghanistan, and Gladys sang her praises. She was a cheerful woman who always brought him a cup of tea and sent him home with cookies.

He never considered his visits to Jonas Finch part of the job. Jonas lived on the north side of the lake and had been friends with Joe's father's old friend, Ben Rumford. Joe often spotted Jonas on the lake in his restored wood boat. Today Jonas had given Joe his catch, two good-size trout, already cleaned and fileted.

After his shift ended, he cooked the fish for himself and Chloe before getting cleaned up and dropping her over at her friend Tabitha's for a sleepover. He was on call, but he'd assured Hunter he'd make it to the surprise engagement party that night.

Chloe had asked about Laurel a couple of times, and he'd brushed off her queries, implying they were both busy. If things continued as they were, he supposed he'd have to come up with an explanation. He had always looked out for the people he cared about. He taught self-defense because he believed in empowering others, especially women, to protect themselves. He was cautious, but considered himself perceptive, and his instincts had saved more than one situation. Not this time.

This time his instincts had led him straight into a mistake, and he didn't know if he could fix it.

"You know how much I love you," he said to Chloe as she got out of the truck in front of Tabitha's.

"I know, Dad," she said before shutting the door. "Love you. Bye!"

He sat there for a minute, watching while Chloe's friend came to the door, and his daughter turned and waved. Chloe took his love for granted. It had always been a given in her life. He'd always been there, always provided and protected. That was the way it should have been for Laurel. The glaring difference between their lives and hers pained him. She'd never had a parent checking up on her, worrying about her, warning her. She'd been her own support.

There were already quite a few people at the Wild Card when he arrived. Twinkling lights hung from the ceiling against each wall. Poinsettias decorated the tables and booths. A floor-to-ceiling tree stood in front of the main window, loaded with lights and decorations.

"What will you have, Sheriff?" the bar owner asked.

"Evenin', Ace. I'll have a cola."

"You must be on call."

He nodded and sat at the bar next to his friend, Jackson, the local vet. "How's married life treatin' you?"

"Kate is great," Jackson said with a grin. "And I never knew how much I'd love being a dad. You probably get it."

"I do," Joe answered. "My girl Chloe makes the sun rise in the morning."

"Kate is talking about putting Madison in dance classes. What do you think?"

"Chloe has loved dance her whole life. It's taught her discipline, and she's made good friends. She already has a scholarship to a dance academy in New York when she graduates."

"I heard she's really good."

"She is."

Jackson took a draw on his tall glass of beer. "So, word is you're seeing someone."

Joe turned his glass in the ring of condensation on the bar. "Laurel Whitaker, my neighbor. She has a contract for web design and all that with the lodge."

"Good for you. Can't even remember hearing rumors about your love life before."

"Never was much to talk about. Don't know if this is either."

Jackson raised an eyebrow. "Not serious?"

"It's serious on my end. I may have screwed it up, though."

"If it's the real deal, you'll work it out."

He hoped so.

"Joe! Jack! Come join us." Gage Ewing, the local doctor motioned them over to his table with Deke and Hunter. Ruby was placing fresh drinks on the table.

"Hey, Joe," she said. "Need a refill? What are you drinking?"

"I'm on call, so cola, thanks."

She hurried away and Joe asked Hunter, "Why is she working? Isn't this the big night?"

His friend shrugged. "She still thinks it's a Christmas party and insisted on helping Ace."

"Maybe we can get a couple hands in before the music gets too loud." Gage shuffled a deck of cards. The interior was filling up with people, but the jukebox was still playing, so the music wasn't too loud.

"I'm game," Joe said and waited for his cards.

"I'm in until Kate gets here," Jackson agreed.

They were betting on a second hand when Jackson's wife, Kate showed up and planted a kiss on his cheek. She greeted the others. "You finish your hand," she said. "I'm going to go say hi to friends."

Deke tilted his head toward a gathering. "Who is that in the blue?"

"Matt Chandler's sister," Hunter replied.

Joe glanced across the room and spotted the young woman they'd mentioned. His heart dipped when he saw who Whitney was with. Laurel wore a slim pair of jeans with black heels and a shiny pink top. Her luxurious black hair fell across her shoulders in loose curls. A deep sense of relief engulfed him. She'd trusted him to keep her secret, otherwise she'd have left Spencer.

"And Laurel Whitaker," Hunter pointed out.

"That's her?" Jackson said from beside Joe.

"That's her."

The band had arranged themselves on the platform and live music blared from the speakers. Within minutes, Kate arrived and led Jackson to the dancefloor.

Crosby arrived and took Jackson's seat. "Hey, big brother."

"Did you come alone?" Joe asked.

"No, I brought mom and her friends." He indicated the ladies carrying drinks from the bar to a booth. Lila Quinn was one of his mom's good friends who was a few years younger, and Rowena Irwin was a widow with two grown sons. The three of them, along with Loydelle Hendershot often went together to activities and always enjoyed fish fries at the VFW on Friday nights.

"Thank goodness they turned off the jukebox or we'd be listening to Elvis all night," Crosby said, and the others chuckled. Loydelle was famous for bringing rolls of quarters and monopolizing the music selection.

"Any trouble tonight," Gage said to Joe and Hunter. "Just let Loydelle swing her purse at 'em."

The men around the table laughed.

Hunter folded and pushed back his chair. "I'm going to give Ace a break and tend bar for a while."

Joe's attention drifted back to the gathering of women who stood chatting, his sisters among them now. They stood near a table heaped with full trays of cookies and candies. He suspected the punch bowl contained spiked cider. Brooke said something to Laurel, and rested her hand on her shoulder. They shared a smile. The gesture touched him, but twisted the ache in his chest as well. Brooke was one of the kindest, most sensitive people he knew. He'd been happy for Laurel to enjoy her company the few times she'd been around his siblings.

Laurel had never had the privilege of a supportive family. Child victim advocates and counselors obviously had her best interests at heart and had done the best they could, but they hadn't loved or nurtured her. It had been a risk for her to become friends with him, with Chloe, to interact with his family. In doing so, she had risked her privacy. He hoped their falling out didn't hurt these tenuous relationships. Laurel needed friends and healthy examples.

Hunter was showing something to his sister, Miranda, who'd recently married an architect from Boston. Jakob and his wife, Willa, who was Jackson's grandmother had arrived as well. Looked like all the Spencers were turning out for the surprise engagement party.

The band took a break and returned. This time Jericho stood up front at the mic. "It's really great to see everyone here. Thanks for coming out. Hopefully this will be a yearly event."

Everyone clapped and cheered. The band played the intro to a popular song.

"We have a special request tonight," Jericho continued. "But before that—" He looked pointedly into the small gathering on the dancefloor.

Attention focused on Hunter and Ruby.

Hunter spoke loud enough for everyone in the room to hear. "I never understood this song until I met you. But now I know. Because there isn't one word to describe how I feel about you. I love you. I need you. I can't live without you. You are my everything."

He dropped to one knee and pulled a jewelry box from his pocket. "Ruby Leigh Dupree, will you marry me and be my love and my life for this lifetime and beyond?"

There was a moment of expectant silence, and Joe didn't hear Ruby's word's, but there were sighs and murmurs nearby. Applause broke out, and Hunter stood to hold his new fiancé close as the music started up. *"You are the candle, love's the flame, a fire that burns through wind and rain. Shine your light on this heart of mine, 'til the end of time.'"*

No one could sing a love song like Joe's deputy. What the talented guy was still doing in Spencer was beyond Joe's comprehension, but Jericho loved his job and was every bit as good at keeping the law as he was at singing.

Joe noticed bunches of mistletoe hanging above the dancefloor and, thinking about the conversation about Christmas movies the other day, he unconsciously pressed a hand to his chest. The last time he'd been here while Jericho sang, he and Laurel had danced to a Keith Urban song she said she liked. He'd held her close, the scent of her hair and skin under his nose, in his head. He'd gone home with her that night....

Everything would have been perfect if he hadn't pressed so hard. Now nothing was right between them.

He scanned the saloon and spotted her.

She'd been looking at him too, and across the room, their gazes locked. Because of all the Christmas lights, the interior wasn't as dark as usual, and her near-black eyes with their fringe of black lashes pierced him with regret. The uncertainty she tried to keep hidden had become obvious because he knew her now.

'Don't come back. Don't call me.'

Those words still twisted his gut.

He loved her.

The song finished and the band played a faster tune.

"I'm going to go catch up on some paperwork," he said to Deke and Jackson over the music. He grabbed his jacket, loaded a paper plate with cookies, slapped another plate over the top and left the Wild Card. Since there'd been a crowd expected, he'd parked at the Sheriff's Department on the other side of the park and walked, so he trudged across Brook Park and let himself into the building.

Deputy Derek Wick was manning the front desk while reading a dog-eared Louis L'Amour paperback novel. Joe set the plate of cookies in front of him. Derek closed the book with a grin and lifted off the top plate. "Wow, thanks, Sheriff! This is a treat."

"Well, it stinks to have night duty when there's a party at the Wild Card."

"I don't mind taking my turn," the fellow with the boyish face told him. "You did your time in the day, didn't you?"

"Sure did."

"This calls for a carton of milk." He got up and went into the breakroom, returning with a blue-and-white quart carton.

"I thought you were going to say cappuccino," Joe said.

Derek shook his head. "Can't stand that stuff."

Joe chuckled. "Good. You're a growing boy." He headed for his office. "I'm not here unless there's an emergency."

"Copy that."

He closed the door and opened a file on his pc. He wanted to write up his wellness reports and not think about Laurel. He hoped she was enjoying herself. She deserved friends. She deserved to not be terrified of being recognized or having her identity exposed. Her worst fear had been discovery, loss of privacy—and he'd blown up her world.

He wished with all his being that he was back at that party with her, holding her in his arms on the dancefloor, seeing her delighted smile, admiring the sparkle in her eyes while she enjoyed a new experience.

She'd learned to be competent and independent by necessity. She'd spent her life on the lookout for threats. Her privacy had been her safety net. Her strength and wellbeing had lain in keeping her secret. Self-preservation was all she knew, and yet beneath it all she craved normalcy. He wanted that for her.

An hour later, the curser still blinked on the form on his screen. He'd come here to occupy his mind and had only thought about Laurel. She hadn't wanted his help. She didn't want or need his pity. She probably had no desire for his love either.

But he'd fallen hard. He was head over heels, single-mindedly, knot-in-his-chest in love with Laurel Whitaker.

CHAPTER FIFTEEN

Kate, the bookstore owner, filled a cup from a silver urn and handed it to Laurel. "Hot cider with dark rum and butter. Have you tried it?"

"Never."

Kate handed her a cinnamon stick. "Stir with this. But they sneak up on you, so if you drink more than a couple, make sure you ask for a ride home."

"Will do."

Laurel was surprised when Jakob came over to speak with her. His wife joined them. Willa's flowing silver-and-bronze dress complimented her silver hair and sparkling violet eyes. "How nice to see you," she said to Laurel. "How are you adjusting to life in Spencer?"

"I like Spencer very much," Laurel told her. "Everyone is friendly and welcoming."

"We have a meeting scheduled for this coming week, don't we?" Jakob asked. "I'm looking forward to seeing what you've come up with for the website and social media."

"He loves social media," Willa teased.

"I don't," Jakob replied with a grimace, "but I know it's important,".

"I only have a couple of kinks to work out, and the updates will be ready to roll." She stirred her hot cider and the spicy aroma filled her senses. "I'm pretty excited to show you and the rest of the marketing team the finished design. Your tech people have been great to work with."

"We only have the best," he said with a wink.

"Drop by my studio," Willa said. "I'm there most days."

"I will." The couple moved along, stopping to hug Dusty and Kendra, reminding her the Cavanaugh siblings were Jakob's great-nephews and nieces.

She hadn't noticed when Joe had left the Wild Card, because she'd been trying not to keep looking at him, but he was glaringly missing from the gathering at the reserved table.

"He left a while back," Brooke said over her shoulder.

Laurel turned. "Was I that obvious?"

"No." She blew on her steaming cup. "He was. He kept watching you like a sad-eyed puppy. Are you all right?"

Not that many people knew she and Joe had been involved, but his family had caught on. Of course, they were curious. "I'm okay."

"This isn't like Crosby and a new girl every other weekend," Brooke said. "That's so common, we don't usually even learn their names, but Joe had never brought anyone to a family dinner. No one since Chloe's mom, anyway, and Chloe's fifteen. It's not like we talked about you behind your back or anything, but we were pretty hopeful this was a thing."

Laurel composed her roiling emotions to keep her expression placid and her voice calm. "I was scared, but I was hopeful too."

"Joe's the least scary person I know," Brooke said. "Now Steph—Steph is scary."

Laurel laughed, but sobered quickly. "I know," she said. "It's me. I...I have issues trusting."

Brooke took a deep breath and glanced at the couples dancing. "I get it. It's none of my business. None of us are going to butt in." She looked back and met Laurel's eyes. "Just know I'm your friend, okay? No matter what happens."

Laurel's throat got tight, and she swallowed back the threat of tears. "Thanks," she managed.

Without possibly knowing how much it would mean to her, but simply out of the kindness of her heart, Joe's sister gave her a reassuring hug. Laurel clung to her for a moment, absorbing the other woman's loving concern. Without realizing it until now, she understood these people had restored her faith in others. She'd resented strangers for so long that she'd given no one a chance.

Not even Joe. She'd kept him shut out, compartmentalized.

Brooke released her and they shared a warm smile.

Stephanie joined them, along with Liz and her friends, to whom Laurel was introduced. Dusty asked her to dance, and then an older gentleman who presented himself as Jericho's dad cut in. Atwood Tanner had been the county sheriff who'd saved Joe's record from being tarnished when his wife shot him all those years ago. Atwood held that position for forty years while training Joe as his replacement and then retiring. He was tall, his brown hair liberally sprinkled with silver, and he sported a rounded potbelly. She immediately liked him. "My boy can sing, can't he?"

"He certainly can."

"In college, he was popular at the county and state fairs, but he chose to be a lawman like his old man."

"He said his sister works at the lodge," she mentioned.

"Bethel," he said with a nod. "She's here somewhere with her mama."

"I'd love to meet them."

"Sure." Atwood led her off the dancefloor in search of his family.

By the time the party started winding down, Laurel couldn't believe she'd stayed as long as she had. She'd enjoyed it, and meeting people had taken her mind away from the gnawing feeling in her stomach, if only for a few hours. Jericho walked her and Whitney to their vehicles and waited while they started their engines.

She waved to him and drove away from Brook Park and headed east along Chickering Road until it turned into Highway Thirty-Four. A light snow was falling, beautiful sparkling flakes in her headlights. The last thing she wanted to do was leave this place, leave the best job she'd ever had, leave the people with whom she was miraculously developing relationships.

She'd given them a chance. She'd given Spencer a chance.

Had she given Joe enough of a chance? As soon as she'd learned what he'd done—actually as soon as he knew the truth, she'd felt as though her life had come crashing down around her. The annoying voice of reason in the back of her mind reminded her he'd been looking out for her.

It was what he did. He took care of people.

If she looked at the situation from an impartial view— which wasn't easy—she understood seeing all the factors together had looked as though she was in danger. Had she been in his place, she may have thought the same thing. He was a man of integrity, a protector. He was a take-charge kind of person, perceptive, cautious. He'd seen signs in her that raised flags about her safety.

He'd had honest intentions.

She turned on her music and found the playlist she'd created a couple weeks ago and had been adding to since. Keith Urban sang, *"And I'm gonna love you like nobody loves you. And I'll earn your trust, making memories of us."*

She remembered Joe patiently showing her how to dance, holding her close. He'd told her she was beautiful, and when they were together, he made her feel beautiful.

He thought she was brave. She hadn't been brave enough to tell him the truth though. Her secret was so profound, so *personal*, she hadn't trusted him with it. She'd been stared at and followed and photographed all her formative years. She didn't want to be a freak show. She didn't want to be the poor little girl who'd seen her mother murdered, been held captive for endless days, and left to die.

'My contentment is not dependent upon external forces or events, but upon me.'

She thought she'd understood what that meant when Dr. Easton had written it out for her and she'd memorized it, but she hadn't. What people knew about her or thought about her wasn't who she was. She wasn't that ten-year-old girl— but she had been.

She had been. That was her experience. It was real. It had happened. She'd survived it. She'd overcome it. She'd built a life in spite of it.

The worst had happened. Joe had learned her secret.

But the bottom hadn't fallen out of the world.

❧

He had barely fallen asleep when the sound of an engine shutting off and someone approaching the Airstream woke him. Barney woofed, but didn't bark.

Joe sat up and scrubbed his hands over his face to clear the grogginess from his head. Were Tiffany's parents bringing Chloe home? They would've called, and besides she'd outgrown overnight homesickness years ago. He raised a slat on the blind beside his bed and peered out.

Laurel's vehicle.

Her knock sounded on the metal door before he could reach it. He leaned down, opened the latch, and pushed open the door.

She stood on the snow-covered ground below, the hood

of her parka pulled around her face, snowflakes falling around her.

"Come in," he said, and backed up.

She climbed the stairs and stretched back to close the door. Barney was right there, sniffing the legs of her jeans and licking the snow from her boots.

"Here," he said, reaching for her coat. "That's wet."

She shrugged out of it, and he hung it on a kitchen hook.

Her cautious dark-eyed gaze raked over his bare chest. "You were sleeping."

"Barely. Have a seat." He gestured to the overstuffed furniture in the living area and padded back to grab his t-shirt from the foot of his bed and pull it on. When he returned, she was perched at one end of the sofa, her knees and feet primly together. "Do you want to take off your boots? They're wet."

"Oh, sorry I got your floor wet."

"Can't hurt this floor. Thought your feet might be cold though."

"They are," she admitted and reached to unzip and remove her knee-high boots. "Is Chloe sleeping?"

"I doubt it. She's spending the night at Tiffany's. They're usually awake all night and sleep the next day." He grabbed a couple of dishtowels, wiped the floor and her boots and set them in the sink to dry. She was wearing a little pair of thin black socks, so he got her some thick gray socks and watched her pull them on.

"Would you like something warm to drink? Coffee?"

She shook her head. "No thanks."

He sat at the other end of the sofa. Barney sat on his haunches and stared at them. "Go lay down, Barney."

The dog went to his cushion and settled in with a grunt.

A minute ticked by before Joe said, "I'm—"

She held up a hand. "Don't say anything. Please don't apologize again."

Laurel lifted her deep dark gaze to his. He wanted to fix this, but he didn't know how. She'd come to his door at nearly one a.m., so that must mean something.

"You said I was brave," she began. "But I wasn't. I was afraid. All the time. I was afraid of being Meryl Greene, the girl behind the headlines. All those years of hiding from the media, years of therapy, years of waiting for something terrible to happen...all that time I was hiding from myself." She dared a glance at him. "It's like I never acknowledged that person was me."

He found his voice. "It's understandable."

She studied her hands on her knees. "My mother had a string of men in her life, and we moved from one place to another, sometimes in the middle of the night. A lot of times during the night, actually. I only remember pieces of my childhood. Therapists say that's a coping mechanism. But I remember that night. I woke up to shouting. That particular boyfriend's name was Monte Swan."

Joe had read about the murder, the kidnapping charges, and the trial. He knew who she spoke of.

"I went into the living room, and I saw him hitting her. Next, she was on the floor, and he kept hitting her. I didn't realize until I saw blood that he had a knife."

"You don't have to tell me this," he said.

"I do," she said firmly. She looked at him. "I have to say these things."

"Okay."

"She wasn't moving. And there was a lot of blood. Monte looked up then and saw me. I ran, but he caught up to me. His hands were slick, and I got away. I ran out the back door and through weeds and tall grass to the neighbor's storm cellar. I knocked over some jars and cut my foot, but I hid there. Sometimes I still smell peaches when I'm scared."

Oh, God. He wanted to cry for her, but he remained still and composed.

Her gaze appeared focused on a shelf of books, but it was obvious she was seeing only that night and reliving the experience. "I thought he'd given up. A long time passed. But I waited, thinking when morning came it would be safe to leave. I knew my mother was dead.

"But he hadn't given up. He found me and tied my ankles and knees together, tied my hands behind my back, then carried me out of that cellar to his car and dropped me in the trunk. He drove a long time. I think I fell asleep for a little while, but then there was a bump and loud sounds, and I was tossed back and forth so hard I was knocked unconscious.

"A lot that happened after that is blurry, because I hit my head. I got hungry. I had to pee. I hurt everywhere."

Police reports recorded the car had overturned more than once, and she wasn't removed from the trunk for a day or more afterward. Joe's temples throbbed from the mental images.

"Eventually he came for me. I thought he was going to kill me, but he carried me into the woods and stayed in a shed with me for a day or two. He gave me a little water, but then he left."

Monte Swan had been driven by his own hunger and need for drugs to abandon her. He'd probably gotten his fix and forgotten about her.

"I don't know how, but James Denning discovered me. I was in bad shape, so I barely remember…."

"Dehydration and blood loss," Joe said. "Infected cuts."

"But I remember seeing the light streaming onto the plank floor when he opened the cabin door. He was very big and wearing a red plaid shirt. He untied me and gave me water. He saved my life."

Joe blinked and managed to say, "I know."

"After what seemed like a long time in the hospital, I was released into state custody. Each time I went out there were always photojournalists. Everyone knew who I was, and it was hard for the foster parents. And then when it seemed as though things would settle down, there was a trial. Monte Swan was eventually given a life sentence. He died in prison."

Her voice had remained calm through the entire telling. "Jim visited me every few months throughout all my school years," she said. "After I had my court records sealed and changed my identity, I contacted him to set up meetings. We still see each other twice a year."

"He seems like a good person," Joe said.

She gave a brief nod. "He is. He lost his wife a few years ago. He has a son. I never met his family. He was just a nice man out surveying land in a remote area, and he happened across me."

"I'm thankful he saved you."

She gave Joe a tremulous smile. "You saved me too. Not from death, but from myself."

"I don't understand," he said.

She slid across the sofa cushions to sit beside him and reached for his hand. Her fingers felt delicate in his grasp. Her eyes were deep and luminous, her black fringe of lashes damp and spiky. "I spent all my energy focused on denying who I was, denying that experience and terrified someone would see the real me. I didn't even know the real me. I became the person I made up."

"Don't you think the person you were and the person you are now are the same?" he asked. "You devised a way to build a new life, to educate yourself, to handle the fear and trauma. You're strong and brave and determined, and that's all you."

"I was afraid to tell you," she reminded him. "Even after you told me your secret."

"I should have waited," he said.

She shook her head. "No. You couldn't have. You were doing what you always do—taking care of someone you believed needed your help." She rested her hand on the front of his t-shirt under which his heart beat rapidly. "You're especially protective of Chloe and your family. I hope I'm one of the people you care about."

He crushed her hand against his chest until she flattened her palm. "You don't know how hard it was to respect your wishes when you told me not to come to your door or even call you. I needed you to trust that I'd do as you asked."

"I trust you, Joe."

"I haven't been able to think of anything but you. Tonight was torture, remembering dancing together, thinking of our night together. Thinking everything we had may have been ruined. At least you didn't leave."

"Of course, I didn't leave." She climbed up to straddle his lap and bracket his face between her hands. "Not when I've only discovered this." She kissed him, and he wrapped his arms across her narrow back, holding her as close as he could without crushing her against him. Her mouth was warm and inviting, and she tasted like apple cider and spice.

He dug his fingers into her hair and held her fast, tasting her, showing her he cared very much about her. She moved fractionally away to press her lips at the corner of his mouth, on his chin, his jaw, to lean up and kiss each of his closed eyelids.

He opened them to study her amazing eyes and dewy lips. "I'm in love with you, Laurel. Passionately, boundlessly—like to-the-moon-and-back in love with you."

Her eyes were wide with questions. "How did I earn the love of a man like you, Joe? What did I ever do to deserve it?"

"You didn't have to earn my love. You're just you, and that's more than enough for me. Just looking at you takes my breath away, but on top of that you're smart and kind and genuine."

"How does it feel?" she asked.

He didn't know if he could tell her. "My chest is so full right now I can't contain the feeling—sort of a combination of excitement and nervousness. Your pain has been my pain.

I'd have happily taken it for you if I could have. When I'm not with you, I want to see you. And when I see you, I'm happy. I feel…I feel like something wonderful is going to happen—all the time." He kissed her. "And it has."

"I probably had trouble separating that excitement and nervousness from the anxiety I was used to," she told him. "I wanted to hide my flaws so you wouldn't find me lacking." She smoothed his hair around his ear. "After I met you, the feeling of doom I've always known faded, and I looked forward to being with you. I think about you all the time, and I want to be with you."

"If you were to analyze those feelings, what would you come up with?" he asked.

"I'd say I was to-the-moon-and-back in love with you."

"You might want to think before you commit. That's seriously in love."

She smiled and kissed him. "I'm seriously in love with you, Joe Cavanaugh."

"I come with a whole passel of noisy, butt-into-your-life family members."

"I'm going to love them too."

CHAPTER SIXTEEN

*C*hristmas Eve with Joe was indeed comparable to a Hallmark movie, and Laurel had no complaints. First, he'd surprised her with a snowmobiling excursion, explaining that it was too cold for the go carts on her bucket list. "But we'll drive go carts in the Spring," he promised.

Stephanie had prepared her for the bitter wind with a special protective salve for her nose and cheeks and a face scarf. After the exhilarating experience, the family changed clothes and spread out in the newly completed great room of Joe's log house. Enormous rugs lay under groupings of comfortable furniture on the recycled wood floors, and though the room was huge, it had a cozy feel.

Grandma Naomi was dwarfed on the comfortable leather chair Crosby had reserved for her. Listening to the conversation around her, she beamed with pleasure.

"How do you all like the throw cushions?" Chloe asked.

The twins and their mother admired every last decorative pillow on all the chairs and sofas. There were several made of fluffy sheepskin, a couple in violet velvet, a few mandala patterns, one with blue mermaid scales, another with a llama face, and others with sayings like, 'This is our happy place' and 'Life is better at the lake.'

"I think someone chose them with great care," Stephanie said.

"Dad let me choose them all," Chloe said with a grin.

Laurel gave Chloe's aunts and grandmother credit for acting as though they were surprised at that information, and shared a grin with Joe. The teen had been thrilled to select those particular accents and to help Laurel with décor fitting the log home.

"I ordered the furniture months ago," Joe told his family. "Laurel helped with a few more choices, and most arrived this week. There are more pieces arriving in January."

"It's all just lovely," Liz told her son and gave him a hug around the waist. "I'm so happy for you." She smiled up at him. "For a lot of reasons."

"The soups are hot," Colette called from the kitchen. "Who wants to eat?"

Joe had designed a kitchen big enough to hold extra folding tables and chairs for additional seating besides the long island and a trestle table and chairs.

They ate steaming rich oyster stew, which Laurel had never tasted previously. Stephanie served long thin imported Italian breadsticks wrapped in paper thin slices of prosciutto and Serrano ham that she'd prepared. A salad of winter greens with vinaigrette, as well as warmed brie with thinly-sliced granny smith apples rounded out the meal.

"This is so different from Thanksgiving dinner," Laurel commented. "But every bit as delicious and filling. Is this a family tradition?"

"Oyster stew was a tradition in my husband's family," Liz told her. "But now each year we think up a new menu to accompany it."

"This never changes though." Colette popped the corks on two bottles of champagne and poured into paper cups.

"We'll have to get you some proper stemware," Stephanie said.

After the meal, they moved back into the great room. The youngsters took seats on the floor around the Christmas tree.

"The tree is perfect," Liz told Joe.

"All I did was set it up. Laurel and Chloe get the credit for the décor."

"We got ideas on Pinterest," Chloe told them.

Most of the ornaments were bobbers and colorful lures. They'd sliced a fishnet and twisted the strips through the branches. The three of them had spent an evening hot-gluing tiny red plaid bows to clusters of varnished acorns and pinecones and finished it off with strings of popcorn.

"It's very clever," Stephanie assured her niece. "I might copy it for the lodge next year."

Ian noticeably bounced up and down where he sat on the floor. His gaze flitted from one adult to the other.

"Go ahead, Ian," Dusty said. "Start passing out the gifts."

His son shot under the tree branches and pulled out one brightly-wrapped package after another. Then he and Kyle read the name tags and handed them to the family members.

Laurel realized what a smart choice it was for the youngsters to go first. They ripped paper and dug into boxes, even the teenagers squealing as they revealed their gifts.

Everyone had a package from Grandma Naomi and paused with them on their laps. "I don't sew anymore, you know," she told them.

"I loved the flannel pajamas you used to make for us, Gram," Brooke told her.

Liz nodded. "I think I have a photo from every year with all of them in their new pajamas on Christmas morning."

"Go ahead." Naomi waved her slender hand.

Even Laurel had a package to open. She untied the ribbon and lifted off the lid. Nestled inside tissue paper was a lovely deep-blue satin pajama set. She held up the top and Joe caught her eye. He grinned.

Ian and the teens all received red plain flannel, the women similar silk sets and the brothers admired handsome bathrobes.

"How did she shop for all of these?" Laurel whispered.

"My guess is Stephanie helped her order the sizes and colors," he replied. "Mine is L.L Bean."

"I don't know if my gift will be appropriate or not," Liz said. "Crosby, will you hand Laurel that present with the white ribbon?"

Crosby found the package his mother indicated.

Unaccustomed to opening a gift with an audience, Laurel warmed with embarrassment. Joe scooted closer to her on the ottoman and gave her a reassuring smile. "It's all right. Go ahead."

Laurel counted, but felt calmer after reaching twelve, so took a deep breath, slid curling ribbon from the box and gently tore the wrapping paper. She'd had a few impersonal gifts from employers, but this was the first time since she'd been small that she'd received things specifically selected for her.

Packed carefully inside the box were shiny glass bead garlands. Laurel lifted them out. Three long strands in reds and greens with silver accents. Her heart skipped a beat. "Oh, Liz."

Glancing up at Joe, she noted his pleased surprise. He shrugged. "I haven't told her," he said softly.

"I hope they'll go well on the tree," Joe's mother said.

"They'll be beautiful," she replied. "Thank you."

"And now I have a gift for Laurel," he said. "She already knows what it is, but we're making this official."

Everyone quieted in expectation.

Laurel's heart pounded nervously. She did know. He'd asked her to marry him two evenings ago. She'd taken a day to think it over, but she really hadn't needed the time. She knew what she wanted more than anything. Yesterday she'd told him yes. He'd kissed her silly and asked her if it would be okay to make it official on Christmas Eve.

Joe extended his palm, which held a royal blue velvet box.

She met his eyes and found all the love and acceptance she would ever need in this lifetime. James Denning may have saved her life the first time, but Joe Cavanaugh had saved her from herself.

She smiled tremulously and counted to twenty before she reached for the ring box. Inside was a sparkling square diamond ring. "Oh," she said on a sigh. "It's perfect."

"So are you." He took it from the box and slid it on her finger. "I love you, Laurel."

With her other hand, she cupped his jaw. "I love you, Joe." She leaned toward him.

"Wait!"

"Hold on there!"

Startled, she turned to see who'd interrupted their moment.

Joe's sisters and Colette urged them from the ottoman and guided them to the doorway to the kitchen. Sometime since their meal, a fat sprig of mistletoe had been fastened to the wood.

A glance showed anticipatory smiles, and Liz waited, poised with her phone to snap a pic.

"I warned you," he said. "You're marrying my daughter and a big crazy family."

"Come on, Dad, just kiss her!" Chloe urged.

"I love your daughter and your big crazy family," she assured him.

The kiss they shared under the mistletoe was a pledge to each other and a promise for the future. She rested her palm over the reassuring beat of his heart. Normal was going to take some getting used to, but she was up for it. She broke the kiss to a sprinkling of applause and turned in his arms to face her new family.

"I have some things to tell you about myself, and now while everyone's together will be the best time."

"And one of the things we have to tell you is that our family might be bigger next Christmas." Joe extended an arm to Chloe. She gave them each a hug and Joe tucked her under his other arm. They'd already talked about this the evening before.

"What?" Liz asked in surprise. "A baby already?"

"Not a baby," Joe told his mom. "Well, maybe, but probably not. Probably an older child. Or two."

The baffled faces of the Cavanaugh family showed their puzzlement, but then Liz nodded as though enlightened.

"We're going to be foster parents," Laurel announced. "Of course, we'll have to be approved, but that shouldn't be a problem."

Liz approached, admired the engagement ring, and gave Laurel a warm hug. "I'm so proud and happy for you both."

Step six was going to be a whopper. Laurel was about to tell this entire room full of people her story. But she wasn't afraid—in fact she was looking forward to it. She could be herself, the new self she'd become, and she'd have their love and support. Nothing had ever felt more right.

"There's more champagne," she said. "Let's sit around the fire, shall we?"

❦

If you've enjoyed Whisper My Name, please leave a review: https://amzn.to/3hl5a5g

ABOUT THE ASPEN GOLD SERIES

Dear Reader,

Once upon a time a group of writer friends—helping a member with a particularly difficult thread in a continuity series contrived by her editors—got the grandiose idea to create a continuity series of their own.

Yes, this was us, and we threw ourselves wholeheartedly into developing characters, fashioning families, family dynamics, and a setting, which evolved from one member's love of all things Colorado. We created family trees, character profiles, detailed maps, brainstormed titles and themes. We collected photos and researched and even started the stories. We proposed our idea to a few publishers and got no traction. So, after a time the contracted books came first, two members dropped out of the group, a couple new ones came and went. But the core group remained.

In a tragic turn of events we lost a beloved friend and co-writer. Grief took the remaining wind from our sails. We recovered slowly, welcomed a new friend to our critique group. Then came a day when we got together and said, "We're going to get serious and do this!" Energy built, and the series took on new life. A previous co-creator joined us again. Now, here we are, years after the initial idea, sharing the finished stories with you and hoping you will feel the same intensity and appreciation for this project as we do. We have many more stories to share, and the ideas keep coming. Look for more books to follow in Aspen Gold: The Series.

So, come along. We welcome you to Spencer, Colorado, to have a look inside the families, to laugh in their good times and cry in their sad times, to follow them as they solve mysteries, expose secrets, recover from their pasts, reach for their goals, and most importantly—as they fall in love.

❦

These Aspen Gold books are independently published by the authors. We thank you for your support, and we take pride in giving you quality books and excellent stories. We're thankful you've chosen to follow us and be part of the AG community.

Reviews help readers discover and connect with new authors. Every review is important to us and is greatly appreciated. Please consider leaving an honest review of this book at your favorite bookseller and Goodreads.

Be sure to follow all the Aspen Gold Series updates at:

Aspen Gold: The Series Website.
https://www.aspengoldseries.com/
Aspen Gold twitter. Https://twitter.com/@gold_aspen
Aspen Gold: The Series on Facebook
https://www.facebook.com/AspenGoldSeries/
Rocky Mountain Rumors, the newsletter
https://www.subscribepage.com/n9n7p3

We love to hear from our readers. Contact the Aspen Gold authors at mailto:rumors@aspengoldseries.com

❧

The Aspen Gold Books

Dancing In The Dark Cheryl St.John
He had everything a man could want--except her forgiveness...
Call Me Mandy Debra Hines
The last man Miranda loved took everything from her...
Ryder's Heart *lizzie starr
She can't allow secrets to steal love from her...
For Keeps Barbara Gwen & *lizzie starr
Hiding the truth is like denying the sun...
Second Chances Donna Kaye
She tried the fairy tale and the fairy tale didn't work...
Sleepin' Alone Bernadette Jones
Hunter Lawe...riding the line between enforcing the law and breaking it...
Stay A Little Longer Bernadette Jones
Death didn't frighten Gage Ewing. Living scared the hell out of him,,,
Speechless *lizzie starr
How many peonies does it take for Vianna and Ryder to get married?
Close to the Heart Debra Hines
He raised her child as his own...
Finding Hope Donna Kaye
Is the peace he's found too good to be true?
Fortunate Cookie *lizzie starr
This woman... wearing frosting... and nothing else...
Lonely Eyes Bernadette Jones
There is an art to pursuit.
Whisper My Name Cheryl St.John
She was the girl behind the headlines

❧

COMING IN 2020

Gorgeous Scars M.A. Jewell

COMING IN 2021

Another Night Alone Bernadette Jones
Maybe I'm The One. Cheryl St.John
Just My Imagination *lizzie starr

ABOUT THE AUTHOR

Cheryl has always loved the exciting and diverse worlds available between the covers of books. As a child she wrote stories & drew covers, then stapled them into little books. She cut all the tiny images from the book club advertisements in the Sunday newspaper & glued them to bits of cardboard so Barbie® had a full library.

Cheryl is the married author of more than fifty books, both historical and contemporary. Her stories have earned numerous RITA nominations, Romantic Times awards & are published in over a dozen languages. One thing all reviewers & readers agree on regarding Cheryl's work is the degree of emotion & believability. In describing her stories of second chances & redemption, readers & reviewers use words like, "emotional punch, hometown feel, core values, believable characters & real-life situations." Reader reviews show her popularity with readers.

The author lives in the Midwest, USA. When she's not writing or spending time with her family, she's checking out garage sales, flea markets & antique malls. Among her collections are teacups & teapots, roosters, chicken kitchen timers, vintage spice tins, wooden recipe boxes, Barbies®, charm bracelets, vintage jewelry, Kokeshi dolls, white stoneware, Delftware, souvenir spoons, Goebel birds, Royal Copley planters, vintage hankies & BOOKS. Cheryl admits she's a bargain hunter with the heart of a hoarder, trying to live as a minimalist. The struggle is real.

Check out Cheryl's website to see an entire listing of all of her books.

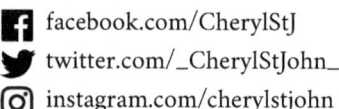

facebook.com/CherylStJ

twitter.com/_CherylStJohn_

instagram.com/cherylstjohn

LINKS

Cheryl's Newsletter Sign up: http://eepurl.com/bqCji9

Aspen Gold Newsletter:
https://www.subscribepage.com/n9n7p3

email Cheryl at: SaintJohn@aol.com

Visit her on the web: http://www.cherylstjohn.net/

BookBub: https://www.bookbub.com/profile/cheryl-st-john

Like her Facebook author page:
https://www.facebook.com/CherylStJ

Twitter: https://twitter.com/_CherylStJohn_

Instagram: https://www.instagram.com/cherylstjohn/

She's a Pinterest junkie!
https://www.pinterest.com/cheryl_stjohn/

Dancing in the Dark

Aspen Gold Series Contemporary

He'd had his own baby. Without her.

Dusty Cavanaugh has loved Kendra Price since she walked into the school cafeteria and captured a dozen boyish hearts with the sweep of her stormy gray-green gaze and the lift of her chin. College, marriage, and children had been the plan. But then Dusty made a mistake.

Kendra Price had never wanted to be rich, but she'd wanted to be comfortable, which she was. She'd never wanted to be famous, but to live her passion to the fullest and dance, which she did. She'd wanted to marry Dusty, have babies and live happily ever after. It would never happen.

She'd wanted to dance, get married and have babies...all she had left was dance.

He had everything a man could want--except her forgiveness...

There had been no road map for life apart. Will love be enough to guide them back?

ORDER FROM AMAZON: https://books2read.com/dancinginthedark-aspengold

Tanner
American Western Historical

He's focused on the future...
The past is all she knows.
Together they're forced to face today.

His months in Salisbury prison taught Union Captain
Tanner Bell to detest a southern drawl, and Widow Cranford's exaggerated Dixie twang has him gritting his teeth. His
plans for a ranch are threatened when his orphaned newborn
niece is delivered to him, and he desperately needs her help.

Raylene Cranford survived a Georgia winter living on
acorns and scrawny rabbits before traveling sixteen-hundred
miles to carve out a life in Colorado. She lost everything--
except her dignity and hope. Her feminine Southern graces
are her armor, but maintaining appearances could cost her
love.

Can a Southern belle and a Union soldier change deeply-
ingrained misconceptions about themselves for the sake of a
child?

ORDER FROM AMAZON: https://tinyurl.com/y5mw5664

Joe's Wife
American Western Historical

Meg's dead husband could do no wrong
Tye Hatcher did everything wrong.... except win Meg Telford's
heart

After Meg Telford's husband dies in the war and is lauded as a hero, she must face the fact that she can't keep the ranch without a man to shoulder the workload. Nothing will stop her from saving Joe's dream. The war has taken nearly all the able-bodied men--and a devilishly handsome bad boy seems her only choice.

Town pariah, Tye Hatcher has a reputation as a hell-raiser, but he's looking to prove himself and has his own plans for the land. Meg's proposal might be too good to be true, but he's willing to take the risk, even if the risk is his heart. Struggling with guilt and the rejection of the townspeople, Meg must learn that her convenient husband is a man who takes risks and does what's right for the sake of others.

Her vulnerable dreams and their hard work will be for naught unless she and Tye reveal their secrets and face what they're both coming to understand--they can't change the past, but the future is in their hands.

ORDER FROM AMAZON
https://www.amazon.com/gp/product/B07TT28FFJ

https://books2read.com/JoesWife

Saint or Sinner
American Western Historical

In this heartwarming tale of redemption, Joshua McBride returns from the war a changed man, ready to put down roots and plant his feet in the community. Prim and uptight Miss Adelaide Stapleton, leader of the Dorcas Society, doesn't believe he's changed—people are never what they seem. But she has plenty of secrets of her own—among them the inescapable fact that Joshua sets her heart to pounding and makes her long for his disturbing kisses. How long can she keep her own past hidden—and resist temptation?

ORDER FROM AMAZON
https://www.amazon.com/Saint-Sinner-Cheryl-St-John-ebook/dp/B00B2Y7OTI/

Land of Dreams
American Western Historical

In this tale of hope and love, too-tall spinster Thea Coulson wants to be a mother to a child who arrives in Nebraska on an orphan train. When Booker Hayes shows up to take his niece, a marriage of convenience suits them both. Thea's nights are filled with dreams of the tall, dark army major, but she guards her heart. Booker's first taste of home and hearth has him longing for more, but first he must win the trust of his niece...and the heart of the sun-kissed farmer's daughter.

ORDER FROM AMAZON
http://www.amazon.com/gp/product/B00B2HFOFG

Heaven Can Wait
Dutch Country Bride Book 1
American Western Historical

Raised within the confines of a strict religious community,
Lydia Beker longs for a simple touch, dreams of seeing more
of the world. When handsome farmer, Jakob Neubauer and
his family visit the bakery where she works, she is fascinated,
but Outsiders are forbidden to her. Jakob is attracted to
Lydia, as well, and she makes the difficult decision to leave
everything she knows behind to marry him. He offers love
and passion, but will she ever fit into his world?

ORDER FROM AMAZON
http://www.amazon.com/gp/product/B00B2HQ1QW

Rain Shadow
Dutch Country Brides Book 2
American Western Historical

Raised by the Lakota Sioux and having traveled with the
Wild West Show for many years, Rain Shadow is unprepared
for a forced stay at the home of Anton Neubauer while her
son recuperates. He is a rock, a man who has lived on and
farmed the same several hundred acres since he was young.

Anton needs a mother for his son, but he needs someone
domestic and ladylike, not the Smith & Wesson toting female
who sets up her teepee in his front yard and whose target
practice wakes him at the crack of dawn. But fate, two little
boys and two old men conspire to keep them together, and
it's too late to deny their passion once love is part of the
equation.

ORDER FROM AMAZON
http://www.amazon.com/gp/product/B00DQ0L7ZS